FEAR NO EVIL

Fear No Evil

First Book of Faith
— Unfolding Chapel Series —

Glennis Tippy

XULON PRESS

Xulon Press
2301 Lucien Way #415
Maitland, FL 32751
407.339.4217
www.xulonpress.com

Paperback ISBN-13: 978-1-6312-9825-7
Ebook ISBN-13: 978-1-6312-9826-4

———†———

I dedicate this story to my New Life Family.
The way you continue to walk your walk of faith,
your walk of love, is forever an inspiration.

———————†———————

Lori really liked Michah and Marcus. "The Boys," as she had fondly nicknamed them, were so different from the men she had hung out with back home. One particular man always came to mind. Devastatingly handsome and sure of it too. He was the reason she was new here. He was the reason she had left everything and everyone back in Pennsylvania.

"He's a very nice young man, Lori." Her boss seemed to know her thoughts. "If I were you, I wouldn't let him get away."

Shaking off the useless thoughts of having him around forever, Lori pushed through the kitchen doors and shifted into work gear. Her thoughts kept circling around to Marcus and his mischievous grin, the feeling of warmth that spread through her from head to toe when he held her hand and kissed it. And she couldn't help but think about how easily their thoughts and minds followed each other. They seemed to be a perfect fit, perfect companions.

Stop! she commanded herself for the millionth time. *You can't keep him. You'll ruin his life just like you ruined your own!*

CHAPTER ONE

———†———

Lori Wright had been in Tulsa a week now. Amazingly, she already had a job and a small, ramshackle two-room apartment. She had food. She had a roof over her head. Life could have been a whole lot worse. She could have been dead. She could have been an accident that was really an unsolved murder.

She surreptitiously studied the two men who sat at the back booth drinking coffee and laughing as they chatted quietly. They were twins. It was obvious. And that, as much as anything, made her curious.

She had figured out that they were both attending the seminary nearby. They both had Bibles and other religious-type books with them. They both bowed their heads and prayed before they ate the food Lori, or one of the other waitresses, placed in front of them.

She could almost tell them apart. Both had dark brown hair and brown eyes behind gorgeous long, dark lashes. The one who came in first every night seemed to be the most outgoing. Lori was pretty sure he was a little taller, and she was positive he was a little more muscular. And even though she thought she could be mistaken, she was pretty sure he had learned which tables she normally waited. Three nights in a row he had walked in, paused just inside the door to look around, and then headed for one of her tables. She found she liked it.

Working a graveyard shift cleaning the bank wasn't Marcus Stout's idea of a good time. But he had to pay his way through school, and he had to go to school. And then there was always homework. He felt blessed that there was an all-night diner—simply called The Diner—across the street so he could get coffee and a roll during his middle-of-the-night "lunch" hour. He could work on his homework then too.

"Boy! That new waitress sure is cute, isn't she?" He could also hang out with his lovably annoying twin brother, Michah, who despite his desire to enter the missions field, seemed never to fail to notice the pretty girls who crossed their path.

Marcus glanced up. Then he did a double take and quickly ducked his head back into his book.

"I saw you look twice, big brother! Don't even try to deny it," Michah persisted.

"Who knew being about eight minutes older than someone would bring so many more years of maturity?" Marcus shot back as he gathered his books and notebooks. "I have to go back to work," he said as he threw a few bucks on the table and headed out the door.

It was a personal best for Michah. It had only taken three nights to get Marcus to notice the pretty waitress.

"Was it something I said?" The new waitress glanced at Marcus's retreating back and then back at Michah. "You are twins." She spoke with certainty.

"And you're very observant." Michah smiled at her. "I'm Michah, by the way," he said. Nodding toward the closing door, he added, "That was Marcus."

"I'm Lori." The pretty blond smiled shyly.

"It's a pleasure to meet you, Lori." Michah stuck out his hand for a handshake. "You're new here, aren't you?" he asked.

"I'm new here. I'm new to this town. I'm new to this state." She heaved a deep sigh and hurried across the room to take an order. She could have kicked herself. *Never give away personal information!* she chided herself.

Michah sat and watched her discreetly for several minutes before he too tossed a few bucks on the table and left. He wondered what her story was. It had not escaped his notice—that brief shadow of fear that paled her cheeks when she turned and hurried away from him and the conversation he had tried to start.

Wow, Marcus thought to himself as he took the elevator up to the fourth floor to finish cleaning the office suite for Mr. Drake, the bank president. *Michah's right; she is beautiful. She looks strong and sweet too.*

When he caught himself thinking about running his fingers through her long blond hair, pulling the ribbon out and letting it flow loose, he chided himself and put his thoughts back in firm control. *Not where a future pastor needs to go*, he reminded himself as he looked in the mirror before he sprayed it down and wiped it clean.

He hummed one of his favorite praise songs from church as he worked. And he thought about the pretty blond waitress across the street—the one with the gorgeous clear green eyes.

He didn't even know her name yet. But he was sure his twin did.

Michah was working his way through seminary as a late shift 911 dispatcher. Marcus attended the same school and worked at the bank. They shared a small apartment in an older neighborhood near the school. Both men had cars but preferred to walk or ride together to save gas.

The Diner was two blocks from the police station Michah worked out of and on the way to the apartment, so most nights he stopped off to visit Marcus for a few minutes. Now he walked the four blocks home, and after spending a few minutes in quiet prayer and reading a few Bible verses, he went to bed. Marcus would finish his shift and be home in a couple more hours.

For Michah the days quietly blended into the nights and weeks became months. He was certain Marcus's life was the same. Michah planned to go into the missions field of ministry and anxiously awaited the day when he would fly off into the unknown to share the Word of God with the unknowing. This was his calling. This would be his life.

Marcus had been called to preach on domestic soil. He would reach the ones who knew but didn't know enough. The ones who were distant from God by their own lack of understanding of the Word, not because they had never heard the Word.

Michah expected to live out his life in simple solitude. Not alone, for his God would be ever present. But he would never expect someone of the fairer sex to commit herself to teaching the unwashed, uneducated, unknowing foreign masses. His hopes for his twin brother were much different. He believed Marcus would fare better with a flock if he had a helpmate. And it was to that end that he studied Lori.

Having been a patron of The Diner for nearly four years, it wasn't hard to figure out the tables each waitress covered. Choosing one of Lori's tables ensured Michah that Marcus would actually see Lori, maybe even talk to her. Marcus would have remained oblivious otherwise.

He had no reason to believe there was anything special, anything different, about her, and yet he did. She stuck in his mind and hung near to his heart as the days became weeks and he slowly got to know her. Marcus got to know her better too.

Lori really liked Michah and Marcus. "The Boys," as she fondly nicknamed them, were so different from the men she had hung out with back home. One particular man always came to mind. Devastatingly handsome and sure of it too. He was the reason she was new here. He was the reason she had left everything and everyone back in Pennsylvania.

She soon found herself looking forward to the twins' nightly visits. She even hoped for a slow night so she had time to chat with them. Even though she needed the tips a busy night would bring her, she also needed the nightly dose of positive affirmation and spiritual guidance. Growing up in church hadn't made her a Christian, but spending time with Michah and Marcus was bringing her closer to God.

"Where do you two go to church at?" she asked one night. "You always sound so sure of God's love and grace. I never got that from the church I grew up in," she added.

"We attend services at the campus chapel," Marcus told her. "You're more than welcome to come with us," he added as an invitation. "Service starts at ten."

"I really don't have any nice clothes for going to church," Lori told them truthfully. She had shared enough of her story that they were both aware of some dire circumstance that had landed her in Oklahoma.

Michah chuckled. "Have you ever seen a college student in a suit and tie?" He shook his head. "Everybody, even Pastor Victor, wears jeans."

Marcus quickly added, "It's not about outdressing anyone; it's about showing up and worshiping God."

And so the following Sunday Lori went to church with the Boys.

CHAPTER TWO

————†————

I t was three weeks until Christmas, and the church was beautifully decorated with a large tree in the back, poinsettias along the
stage, and long strands of soft, white lights hanging down from the
ceiling along the back wall of the stage. It took Lori's breath away.

"This is beautiful!" she whispered to Marcus as she walked
beside him down the center row to some seats near the middle. "We
never decorated at the church I grew up in," she added.

The last comment was spoken so softly Marcus wasn't even
sure she realized she had said it out loud at all. "Christ's birth is
reason for a huge celebration, don't you think?" Glancing over at
her, he saw the small nod of her head.

"Yes. It is." She spoke clearly this time, and another glance
afforded him a huge smile, something he found he really enjoyed
seeing and rarely saw at all.

The three had barely taken their seats when everyone was asked
to stand for prayer. Then the praise and worship team started singing
Christmas carols. Lori's soft soprano readily joined in. She could
hear Marcus's baritone and Michah's tenor ringing out clearly to
her right. Marcus was beside her, and occasionally his arm would
brush against hers, sending a tingle of awareness through her.

She found herself head over heels, overboard attracted to him.
She gave herself a stern and silent lecture. *You just need to stop
right now! You have no right, no business, thinking or feeling this
way! You'll just get in his way and ruin his life!*

A wave of nightmarish memories flooded through her mind and
Lori fought to push them away and enjoy the service.

Marcus couldn't help himself. He had accidentally brushed against her arm while they sang the first Christmas carol. The tingle that shot through him threw him completely off balance. Was he imagining it? Was it static electricity brought on by dry air and carpeting? He brushed against her again, and again he felt that tingle. When he realized he was still doing it and still feeling that strange tingle, he felt his cheeks flush and took a small step away from Lori.

She intrigued and excited him in ways he never thought possible, ways he felt guilty feeling. He knew she had stolen into his heart. And he wondered where her heart was in this growing friendship. She was more talkative when Michah was around, but that was probably just because Michah was more talkative.

After the service, it seemed the most natural thing in the world for the threesome to gravitate to The Diner for lunch. Conversation ebbed and flowed as they ate their sandwiches.

Michah excused himself as soon as he finished eating. "I really need to do some studying for that exam tomorrow." He said.

"Revelations getting the better of you, bro?" Marcus chuckled.

"Yeah. It is. But I will ace the test. God always does His part. I just need to do mine." And with a casual salute, he left The Diner.

Finally Michah had a chance to leave Marcus alone with Lori. The man just wasn't talkative enough. Michah knew his brother and Lori would find plenty to talk about with him out of the way. Both Marcus and Lori seemed to count on Michah to keep a conversation going. He was the more outgoing twin. He knew Marcus would be able to pastor a church and talk to his flock; he just wasn't very good at carrying on conversations with the woman Michah was sure his brother was head over heels in love with.

Lori and Marcus sat in silence for a few moments. Marcus found himself tongue-tied. Lori both intrigued and baffled him. She was, in his eyes, the most beautiful woman he had ever met. And even though he really knew very little about her, he felt he had known her in his soul forever. The feeling unsettled him.

Lori knew she was hopelessly in over her head with Marcus. He was so handsome, so kind, and such a gentleman. She knew he would make a wonderful Pastor. The people who went to his church would see what she saw and love him too.

"So are you going to ace your midterms too?" she finally asked.

"That's my plan," he answered, smiling. Hesitantly he added, "Michah has to work tonight. I don't. I feel like I have plenty of time to go through my notes again later."

Then a thought came to him, and before he had time to chicken out, he asked, "Do you work tonight?"

"I'm off tonight too," she told him. "I'm on here at four tomorrow afternoon. But I have to be at my housecleaning job at 7:30 in the morning." She sighed. "That's a six-hour job."

"Can you spare an afternoon?" he asked. "I'd like to just walk around and enjoy the season." He shrugged, wanting to appear casual even though he was very nearly panicking. He could not believe he had been brave enough to ask Lori to spend the afternoon with him. Had he just asked her for a date?

"That actually sounds nice," she answered. Smiling, she added, "I need to do a little shopping. Do you mind?"

"Of course not. You plan to hit the grocery store? Michah would be really surprised if I did the grocery shopping!" Laughing, they left The Diner and strolled up the street toward the center of town. Marcus somehow managed to keep the smile that stayed on his face from turning into a very loud and happy laugh.

There were lots of little shops around. Most of them were specialty stores selling handmade jewelry, crafts, or paintings by local artists. They wandered into a little resale shop and Lori immediately spied a small Charlie Brown Christmas tree. Marcus could see how badly she wanted it, but she set it back on the shelf and walked around looking at a few other things.

"Will you be going home for Christmas?" Marcus asked, and then, as soon as he saw the sad look flit across her face, he wished he hadn't.

"No," she answered as casually as possible. The lump that had formed in her throat very nearly kept her from speaking at all. "What about you and Michah?" she wanted to know a few moments later, having managed to swallow the lump. "You've never said where your parents live?" It was a question.

"Our parents are both in Heaven now," Marcus told her in a soft, nearly reverend voice. "Father God took them both home about two years ago."

"I'm sorry," she said simply. She wondered at how selfish they must think her for never having asked them about their family. It was just too hard to talk about families at all. "We've never really talked about our families," she said. And Lori figured she probably never would talk about hers.

Marcus shrugged. "It's hard to have much of a conversation at all when you're working and Michah and I just have our break time." He gave her an out.

Now she felt she needed to know more. "What happened? You make it sound like you lost them both at the same time."

Taking a moment to gather his thoughts, Marcus sighed and then told her, "It was late February. They had gone to Kansas City for the weekend, to visit my grandmother. The weather turned nasty and the roads got bad and the drivers got worse. A car was going too fast and whipped in, in front of a semi, causing the semi to jack-knife. The back end of the trailer caught Mom's little sedan and . . ." He trailed off, shaking his head, unable to finish.

"Marcus, I'm so sorry." Lori put a hand on his arm and looked up into his dark brown eyes. She had never noticed the flecks of gold in them. They were eyes she could easily lose herself in.

"Thank you," he said. "Michah and I know we will see them again someday. We're both good with that." He smiled.

"So can I ask about your grandmother?" Lori asked hesitantly.

"She had Alzheimer's. We told her what happened—that her daughter had died. We didn't think she understood, but a couple months later, she told Michah and me that she was going to go home to see Caroline. Caroline was my mother's name. That night she went to sleep and never woke up on this side of Heaven again." Marcus smiled through watery eyes. "She went home to see Caroline."

Lori wasn't sure what to say, so she just squeezed Marcus's arm in a tight hug. He patted her hand and turned those gorgeous, gold-flecked brown eyes on her and smiled. She was sure he understood what she could not find words to say.

"Do you need to pick up very many groceries?" he asked, changing the subject, as they pushed open the door to what was probably the last remaining mom-and-pop grocery store in the country.

"Just a couple of bags." She glanced at him. "Why?"

"Well, we are only about a block from where I live and I thought, if you don't mind, I'd dash over and get the car. I could really stock up and give you and your groceries a ride home as well."

Grinning from ear to ear, she practically shoved him back through the door. Giggling, she told him, "Step on it! If I buy ice cream, it better not melt while I wait on you!"

Laughing a deep, throaty chuckling sound, Marcus sprinted down the street. But before he retrieved the car, he swung back into the resale shop and bought a small Charlie Brown Christmas tree.

Marcus was head over heels, and he knew it. He wanted to lasso the moon and give it to Lori. He wished he could give her so much more than the little five-dollar tree. Would she be upset that he had bought it for her? She seemed to be more and more relaxed and comfortable with him and Michah, but she was still hesitant and keeping them mostly at arm's length. It had greatly surprised him when she shoved him out of the store. That was the most relaxed and comradely she had ever behaved. He would take it as a good sign.

Why did she push him out that door? She was flirting. That would never do. She could still feel the warmth and the strength of his arms. Her hands still tingled from that brief, oh-too-bold con-nection—a connection she had no business making. She could not, would not, lie to the Boys, but she couldn't risk them learning the truth either. *Just stop!* she ordered herself firmly.

And after hearing about what had happened to their parents, Lori found it hard to feel sorry for herself. The double tragedy of losing both of them together, and then their grandmother, must have been horrible and overwhelming.

At least her family was still alive. She hoped so, anyhow. She realized she would have no way of knowing if anything did happen to them.

Marcus seemed at peace with knowing he would see them all again in Heaven. Lori prayed for the peace that knowledge would bring to her. Her family was good people, but they didn't have the close, personal relationship with God that she knew Marcus and Michah had.

After wandering aimlessly around for five full minutes, Lori shook off her angst and started picking up the few things she could afford. She was blessed to be a waitress since it meant she got a good meal every shift she worked.

The owner, Tonya Willis, expected her employees to eat one meal there every shift. It was always the special. It was always good. Lori had been told she was expected to recommend the choices on the menu based on her personal knowledge of how they tasted. Considering she made less than minimum wage, and tips were seldom large, she was happy to comply. She suspected her boss knew her waitstaff would starve without the free meal.

Lori was still pushing her cart around the little store when Marcus returned. "Did you miss me?" he asked, grinning, as he pushed his cart up beside her.

"That was fast," she told him, ignoring his teasing question. No way would she tell him she had been so busy *missing* him she had almost forgotten to shop.

They laughed and joked and Lori forgot not to flirt while they finished their grocery shopping. She caught herself batting her eyes at him and touching his arm in a most possessive sort of way. The harder she tried to get herself under control, the more out of control she felt. *Dear Lord in Heaven, please, please help me not to do this. Marcus needs to not be around me. I need to stop encouraging him*, she prayed sincerely.

Apparently God wasn't listening, because when Marcus said he wanted to spend time with her again, she said yes, that she would like that too. And once she said it, knowing it was true, seeing how he smiled at her, she couldn't take it back.

After parking in front of the old tenement house Lori's apartment was in, Marcus walked her to the door. Longing to kiss her good night, knowing it was too soon, he took her hand and brought it to his lips. It was a cold, chapped hand, and it was so small and delicate in his big paw. He never wanted to let it go, never wanted her to walk through the door into that ramshackle old house. He kissed her fingers, bid her good night, and turned and walked back to his car.

When Marcus got home and started telling Michah about his day, he remembered the tree. Frustrated with himself because he had forgotten to give it to her when he dropped her off, he decided to take it to her before he went to work the next evening. If he hurried, he could get home from his last class, get the tree, and be at The Diner when she got there a little before four. Surely her boss would let her keep it in the back wherever she put her coat and purse. And it wouldn't be too heavy or awkward to carry home when she got off.

Decision made, he popped a frozen pizza in the oven and got his notes out to study a bit while it baked.

"She really likes you, Marcus." Michah spoke to him out of the blue. Marcus wasn't surprised, as the two had always had a knack for knowing each other's thoughts, and Marcus couldn't stop thinking about Lori.

"She's as skittish as a colt, but I don't think it's because she's shy." Marcus looked up at his brother. "Today she was flirting with me one minute and holding back the next." He shook his head. "Something bad must have happened to make her so afraid to open up." Sighing deeply, he added, "I'm crazy about her and terrified I'll scare her off."

Marcus continued, "After we graduate, we'll be leaving. Then what? If I manage to get close and then leave, she's gonna be hurt, and maybe not for the first time either." Michah could feel his twin's frustration as Marcus scrubbed a hand across his face and looked at him, desperately searching his face for an answer.

"All I know, bro, is God put her here where we are for a reason. He will work through the details on His timetable." Giving Marcus a brief, brotherly hug, Michah sat down at the small kitchen table and bowed his head in prayer. Marcus joined him, and as they ate, the conversation turned to more mundane things: school, midterms, applications for pastoral positions and open spots in the missions field.

CHAPTER THREE

———†———

L ori hurried through the door of The Diner and headed straight for the swinging doors to the kitchen. She wasn't late, but she wasn't as early as she liked to be. She would barely have time to put her things away, tidy her hair, and don her apron.

"Excuse me, miss, I think you forgot something." A familiar voice spoke and she whipped around to see Marcus hurrying toward her with a Charlie Brown tree—*the* Charlie Brown tree—held out toward her. "I know you're running late. So am I. But I want you to have this. He clasped her wrist and gently closed her fingers around the tree's base, making sure she held it firmly.

"Oh! But . . . what? Why?" She stuttered and tried to start again.

"Because," he said simply. Shrugging his shoulders, he tipped his hat and turned to walk away. "Merry Christmas." He glanced back and grinned mischievously before opening the door and exiting the building, turning right to head to the crosswalk and across the street to the bank.

Lori stood and stared at the door, speechless. Marcus bought her the tree? Why?

"He's a very nice young man, Lori." Her boss seemed to know her thoughts. "If I were you, I wouldn't let him get away."

Shaking off the useless thoughts of having him around forever, Lori pushed through the kitchen doors and shifted into work gear. Her thoughts kept circling around to Marcus and his mischievous grin, the feeling of warmth that spread through her from head to toe when he held her hand and kissed it. And she couldn't help but think about how easily their thoughts and minds followed each other. They seemed to be a perfect fit, perfect companions.

Stop! She commanded herself for the millionth time. *You can't keep him. You'll ruin his life just like you ruined your own!*

"Can I get more coffee, please?" A soft voice spoke.

"Sure, Mr. Tam." She smiled at the elderly gentleman and brought the pot over to refill his mug.

"Miss Lori." Mr. Tam spoke softly. He always spoke softly. Lori looked at him and smiled indulgently, waiting for him to finish his sentence. "Whoever he is, and I think I know, he must be very special." Mr. Tam smiled and took a sip of his coffee.

Lori just shook her head and walked quickly away. She had to get her focus back here, on The Diner, where it belonged!

"She liked it! She really liked me surprising her with that little tree!" Marcus was pleased with the results. He had worried to Michah last night that Lori might get mad at him for presuming to buy it for her.

Michah grinned at his brother. "Told you so!" he said and chuckled before ducking the pillow Marcus threw at him.

Michah had quickly set him straight. "Women like surprises," he had told his brother. "If you were to go out and buy something really expensive, like jewelry, she would probably be upset because that would imply the relationship is serious."

Marcus had started to protest that he was serious, but Michah held up a hand to stop him. "You are both serious—about getting to know each other well enough to know if you can have a serious relationship." Then he added, "She will love the tree and the thoughtfulness behind you giving it to her."

Charles Arnold was angrier than he thought he ever had been before or would be again. Lori had just vanished into thin air. He thought perhaps the witness protection system had taken her in.

"It's all her cop brother's fault!" he whined to himself. "Detective Wright, you will get yours." He punched the newspaper picture of Lori's brother accepting his detective badge. "I'll find her!" He spoke vehemently. "And you'll both pay."

None of his team was left, so Charles had needed to find a new team. It was hard work handpicking two men whom he knew he could count on, two men who knew enough to keep their mouths shut, two men who enjoyed money enough to work for it.

This time, he would have one of his men driving. He had thought having Lori take them to the airport was the perfect plan. And it would have been if her big brother the cop hadn't stuck his nose in it!

It took him a month, but he found a couple fellows he was confident he could count on. In the meantime, he planned his next two bank robberies.

And he had found another woman to wine and dine and drive him around. It made it so much easier to scope out his next job if he looked like every other innocent man sitting at the restaurant, dining with a beautiful—and very naive—woman.

Restaurants, theaters, small shops, things like that were perfect places to hang out and scope out the banks he wanted to rob. He chose his banks based on what was nearby that he could just hang out in and observe the traffic in and out of the big, old buildings. Older buildings were the only ones he could crack the vaults open in. They were the only ones that ever had older safes that you could open by listening to the combination clicks with a simple stethoscope.

It was dangerous to stay in Pittsburgh, but he grew a beard, changed the color of his contacts, and never went to any of the places he had been before. He changed his name again too. He became Cameron Nash.

He felt like he was slumming when he took his new girl to the movies and then to a cheesy dive that was famous for their burgers and fries, but it got him the information he needed.

The next night, it was pizza and bowling. He hated bowling, but he could not roller skate and had no desire to risk breaking something trying. That would totally mess everything up.

This new girl wasn't as pretty as Lori. No one was as pretty as Lori. But she didn't come with a cop for excess baggage and she worked in the library next door to the bank he planned to hit next. He could wait for her to get off work and observe the bank traffic just by standing near the window. So simple.

Even better, when he accompanied her to the bank with the deposit from the library. She explained to him that they rarely needed to make a deposit, but late fees and occasional donations did eventually add up. His donation helped that process along.

Then he took her out to some really cheesy places that were near the fifth, and final, Pittsburgh job.

Since it was her payday, he got to go inside that bank with her as well. How convenient.

By the time he had all the info gathered for the next two—the last two—jobs in Pittsburgh, he had a new team in place. And this time he had a real getaway driver.

His girl would drop him off, allegedly for a late-night meeting in the bar of the hotel across the street. From there she could take herself home or wherever she wanted to go.

Three days later, and at least one more totally boring date later, he would have her drop him off across the street from his last job. It was an all-night copy and business center. He would disappear inside and exit through the back door. Hopefully by the time he walked around to the front of the building, she would be long gone.

He stuck a fresh stick of gum in his mouth and chewed. Eventually his ears would pop, signaling that he would be able to hear those clicks that meant the safes would open. He hated sinus problems.

The conversation with the Boston PD had not been as rewarding as Detective Todd Wright had hoped it would be. Information on the five bank robberies there was sketchy. He and his Boston contact both thought it was the same ring. The modus operandi—MO—was the same. All the banks had older vaults with combination locks. Apparently someone in the ring, most likely Charles Arnold, knew how to open those old locks. They wore masks and they wore gloves. There was nothing distinctive about their clothes. Their hair and their skin were always covered.

Todd had six years of experience on the force, but being a newly minted detective was making him push harder for answers. He felt he needed to prove himself. The fact that he had been chosen for the job because of how good at the job he had already proven himself to be wasn't holding water for him. And being very near the fine line of "conflict of interest" was making him push harder too.

Even though his gut was telling him all eight robberies, five in Boston and three in Pittsburgh, were related, he still could not prove it. The dots were not connecting.

A night watchman had been shot at the last robbery, and later died in surgery. Now it was not just robbery; it was murder. It made Detective Wright mad.

It was quite by accident, but he didn't care how he found her— only that he had. One of his new hires was Facebooking when they were supposed to be planning the first job together. "Hey, Cam, you gotta see this. It's really funny." He had pestered Charles Arnold, aka Cameron Nash, into looking at the silly video some old friends of his had taken at some little eating joint out in Oklahoma.

"Hold it!" Cameron spoke sharply. "Back it up a bit," he ordered. The man restarted the clip and paused when Nash said, "Stop. There." He took the phone from his hand and stared at the picture. "Looks like I'm gonna be going to Oklahoma" was all he said before he dropped the phone on the table and left the room.

Chapter Four

━━━━━✝━━━━━

L ori looked around her sparsely furnished apartment realizing, not for the first time, that the Charlie Brown tree was the only decorative touch in the rooms. The tree held a spot of honor in the middle of the small table Lori sat at when she ate her meager meals. Today breakfast was two pieces of toast made from the heels of her last loaf of bread and what little grape jelly she could scrape from the jar. It was enough. She had enough tip money to walk to the grocery store today and pick up a few things.

She hadn't been since she and Marcus had shopped together on Sunday. She smiled at the memory. He was such a nice man—kind and thoughtful. Nothing at all like Curtis Maquire. Shaking her head, she knew she would never be able to call him by his real name, Charles Arnold.

Getting up from her little table, she washed her plate and knife. Taking a long drink of water, she wished she could afford coffee, tea, milk, and juice all at the same time instead of needing to choose one or the other. Today she would buy orange juice.

It was a cold morning, and walking to the store made her aware—and quickly—of how badly she needed warm boots. Remembering the pair she had left, forgotten, in the hall closet of her parents' house—her home—brought on a wave of nostalgia. Tears welled up in the corners of her eyes. Shaking her head, she fought back the tears before they spilled over, took a breath, and increased her pace. A brisk walk on a brisk day. Tomorrow, when she got her paycheck, she would go to the resale shop and splurge on a pair of warm boots.

Marcus spent a good deal of his Christmas break hanging out with Lori. She started going to church with the Boys every Sunday.

And she and Marcus went for more than one long walk together. He found he enjoyed her company more than he had ever enjoyed the company of any woman he had ever spent time with. They talked about everything, and they thought alike about almost everything they talked about.

Lori was sweet and kind. She had a beautiful smile. Marcus enjoyed learning how to coax it from her. Sometimes, most times, that was hard to do. It slowly seemed to be getting easier, though. And Marcus felt the effort was most definitely worth the reward.

"What do you plan to do after graduation?" Lori asked Marcus one evening as he sat at his usual table during his work break. Michah hadn't been able to get away from the station yet and The Diner wasn't busy at the moment.

"I'm applying everywhere I think there might be an opening," he told her. "I'll pastor wherever God sends me." Grinning that cute dimpled grin that made Lori's tummy do flip-flops, he added, "Someplace with no winter would be great, though," as he looked out the window at the ice-laden crystals beating down from the sky.

Lori followed his thoughts. "Yeah, I guess Michah's staying pretty busy with the phones tonight." She followed his thoughts a lot. He was used to it with his twin, but coming from Lori, it still unnerved him. He found he kind of liked it, though. He was also discovering that he was learning to read her too, though not as well as she read him and not as well as he read his twin. But he really liked this process of discovery they were going through together. He enjoyed everything he was discovering about her.

Marcus looked at Lori, her blond hair pulled back in a ponytail. She looked so young and innocent. But having gotten to know her over the past few weeks, he knew there was a loss of innocence in the depths of those sparkling green eyes.

"How much longer do you plan to stay here and"—he rotated his index finger in a circle—"do this?" he asked.

Shrugging, Lori rose and turned to walk to the register. "As long as it takes" was the only answer she could give him. And it made no sense to Marcus.

Lori was so smart and kind and sweet and beautiful. He wanted her to have a better life than waiting tables and cleaning houses would ever give her. But he sensed she wasn't interested in doing anything else, anything more. He couldn't understand why, and she always managed to avoid answering his questions about her future plans. What—or who—was she hiding from? The little he knew of her past was that she had fled from Pennsylvania with barely enough time to pack a few clothes.

He sensed she had led a totally different life from the one she led now—if not unconcerned, then at least somewhat sheltered. If not wealthy, then at least somewhat privileged. The winter coat she wore was stylish and warm. The boots, he knew, were from the resale shop, and even though they were a little big, they did keep her feet warm. Laughingly, she joked about wearing an extra pair of socks to keep them on her feet.

Her clothes, jeans, and sweaters were nice too. He had been in her rooms a couple times now, briefly. The tree was the only decoration she had, and he was glad he had given it to her. There were no pictures of family or friends, no decorative touches, no books. She didn't even have a cell phone. He had decided to give her a cheap burner phone for Christmas. He wanted to be able to talk to her when he couldn't see her. He wanted to hear her voice and see her in his mind's eye.

He intended to get to know everything about Lori. She was the most beautiful and intriguing woman he had ever met.

Lori thought long and hard about what to give the Boys for Christmas. She really couldn't afford to give them anything, but she wanted to. It wouldn't feel like Christmas at all if she couldn't buy a few gifts.

She thought about her parents and her older brother and little sister. She missed them desperately and she was sure they worried about her. It had been her brother Todd's idea for her to disappear. Her dad had helped make it happen, but no one knew where she went. Not even her dad's friend Chuck knew, and he was the one who had flown her out of Pennsylvania.

His little plane had taken her to Atlanta. From there she had paid cash for a bus ticket to Memphis, and from Memphis to Dallas. In Dallas she had taken a taxi to the airport, then another to the Amtrak station. Then the train ride to Oklahoma City and the bus to Tulsa.

There had been no real rhyme or reason for any of the places she went that had landed her in Tulsa. And she knew that was the way it was supposed to be.

Chuck had chosen Atlanta for reasons of his own. The bus that took Lori to Memphis left within minutes of her arriving at the ticket counter.

She had used a payphone at the bus station in Memphis and made a brief phone call to her brother. Her brother, the detective, quickly told her that the bank had indeed been robbed and the security guard had died. Then he told her that their facial-recognition equipment had recognized her boyfriend, Curtis Maquire, as Charles Arnold. He was a very dangerous man. A man with many aliases.

When Todd told her Curtis, Charles Arnold, had gotten away, she sorrowfully said good-bye and hung up the phone. The plan was she would keep running and hide. So she caught another bus to Dallas. She had cried the whole long trip there.

There was a vacant taxi at the curb when she walked out of the bus station in Dallas, and someone had asked if they could share it for a ride to the airport. Saying "yes" was the easy answer. And as she had too much luggage to fly, after she got to the airport, she caught another taxi ride and wound up on an Amtrak to Oklahoma City.

She had thought about staying in Oklahoma City, but when she looked at the apartment rental ads in the Oklahoma City newspaper, she knew she couldn't afford them. When she looked at a map of Oklahoma that was hanging on the wall, Tulsa jumped out at her and she felt inexplicably drawn to it, so she did the only logical thing to do: she bought a ticket and went there.

She had spent almost all of her cash on the trip, so as soon as she left the bus station, she found a cheap hotel room, took a shower, put on clean clothes, and went job hunting.

Walking past The Diner, smelling the food, her stomach growled. Realizing she hadn't eaten since the day before, she had looked longingly through the window. Then, spotting the *Waitress Wanted* sign, she had walked in and treated herself to the best burger she had ever eaten. When she inquired, God had immediately blessed her with the waitress job at The Diner. And then Tonya, her new boss, had helped her find an apartment and a couple houses to clean.

CHAPTER FIVE

---✝---

Thinking of Curtis made her shudder. She still remembered the romantic evening when he had told her he would never let her go. Now she wondered if it was a threat. And was he making good on it? She hadn't felt the creepy feeling of being watched or followed. She had expected to feel that ever since she left Pennsylvania. But just because she didn't feel it didn't mean it wasn't happening.

Pushing her feet into her boots, she locked her door and headed down the street to the market. She couldn't stop herself from looking at everyone, and everywhere. She hadn't felt fearful in the several weeks past. Why now? Was it because she had been thinking about it and managed to frighten herself? Or was God trying to warn her that Curtis had found her?

She could feel someone's eyes on her. The hair on the back of her neck stood up. Glancing around as casually as possible, looking in store windows at the reflections of the other people and the traffic on the street, she decided it was all her imagination. It had to be.

Shivering from more than just the cold, she hurried down the street. Christmas was only four days away. How she wished she could contact her family and let them know she was okay, tell them about Marcus. Where did that come from? And why? There was nothing to tell. He was a good man. She was comfortable with him and Michah and sure she could trust them. But she couldn't tell them her secrets. They would want nothing to do with her if they knew what she had done . . . what she had almost done.

Curtis had been so sweet and thoughtful. And he was gorgeous! She had thought him the perfect man when they started dating. That little thing about him not being a Christian had nagged at her. And she had tried to get him to go to church with her, but he refused. Well, not exactly. He had always found an excuse, something else he needed to do. Lori bought it all. At least for a while.

Then came the night when he had asked her to pick him up outside the bank at midnight. When she asked him why, he had said something about a meeting and nothing else. He had been very evasive. For some reason she had mentioned it to her brother.

Todd had just made detective on their local police force. He was in the middle of trying to crack open a bank robbery organization. When Lori mentioned it to him, warning bells went off and he sat her down and questioned her intensely. Thinking about it now, Lori shuddered. She had been seriously involved with a bank robber. And perhaps a murderer, because the night watchman had died during the robbery she had almost helped with. After Todd had told her about it, she had gone through every paper that had been left at The Diner. She had read the whole story in a newspaper someone had left behind. No, Marcus would want nothing to do with her if he knew.

Needless to say, Todd had not allowed her to pick up Curtis. Her car had been parked in the bank's parking lot, near the back door where Curtis had asked her to wait for him. A female officer, dressed in the clothes Lori would have worn and carrying Lori's cell phone, sat in the driver's seat and waited. One of the robbers had been apprehended. One had been shot and died later at the hospital. The night watchman had died too. Curtis had gotten away. Lori had been put on Chuck's plane and whisked away that very same night.

Lori wandered into a used bookstore and began browsing around, thinking maybe she could find a couple books to give the Boys for Christmas. She had never given a used gift before in her life and shuddered at the thought of it now, but it was the best she could do, and she knew Marcus and Michah wouldn't mind.

She ended up finding a book of pulpit jokes for Marcus and a couple children's Bible story books for Michah. Perhaps he could use them to teach the children in whatever country his missionary ministry led him to. She hoped they would be helpful.

As Lori stood waiting to check out, she noticed a pile of brightly colored wrapping paper near the counter. A handwritten sign said, *FREE. Please take only what you need for your purchase today. Thank you.* Seeing two of the customers in front of her taking a sheet and carefully folding it to fit inside the bag with their purchases, she looked upward and whispered "Thank you!" before picking a sheet for herself. Now, she could wrap their gifts.

Tulsa, Oklahoma, was a hick town as far as Charles Arnold was concerned. He'd be glad to see the city lights fade away as he flew out of there. But he had business to take care of first. Taking Steve with him from Pittsburgh wasn't the smartest thing he had ever done, but he needed an introduction to Matt Simpson. He needed to find Lori. And according to Steve, Matt grew up in Tulsa and knew his way around. Charles figured he could drive the getaway car.

"Matt. You're positive Lori still works at this Diner place?" Arnold, aka Conrad Meyer, wanted to know.

"Yeah. I was just in there yesterday and she was there." He had to add, "She was all snuggled up to some guy with a Bible like he was gonna give her a free ride to Heaven." He snickered.

Matt had figured out that the twins she was always hanging around were old buddies of his from when his daddy was a preacher. Mark and Mike Stout. He knew they had fancier names, but he didn't care. He had never cared. And now he was walking right past them and they didn't even know him. He decided he needed to be careful and keep it that way. He could tell his new boss, Conrad Meyer, had big plans for him. He already wanted him to keep an eye on Lori. He wanted to know where she lived and what she drove to work.

It only took Matt a few days to discover Lori didn't drive. She walked everywhere she went unless the twins took her someplace. He followed them to church on Sunday morning, but he didn't go in. He would never darken those doors again!

"Hey, boss! That Lori chick doesn't have a car. She walks everywhere unless those two twin guys take her someplace," Matt told Charles. "They went to church this morning. And she's got a couple of rooms on the second floor of an old tenement house a couple blocks from The Diner." Matt rambled on about seeing her go to one of her cleaning jobs and following her down the street to the grocery store.

"Yeah, okay, I get it." Charles shook his head in exasperation. Matt was even dumber than Steve, and he hadn't thought that possible. "We need to make some plans," he told them, and pulled a small notebook from his shirt pocket.

The Diner was open on Christmas Day from noon until 4:00. Tonya was running the kitchen and everything was set up buffet-style. The employees and their guests, the daily regulars such as Mr. Tam, and any homeless people who happened to wander by were invited to partake of a feast. There was ham and turkey, mashed potatoes and gravy, dressing, candied yams, scalloped corn, pea salad, green bean casserole, Jell-O, pumpkin pie, apple pie, rolls, coffee, and tea.

Christmas carols played all day on the radio, and Lori caught herself singing along as she bused tables for her boss. She didn't have to work very much, though. Three other waitresses were there with their families, and everyone was pitching in. The building rang with laughter.

Mr. Tam wrapped an apron around his waist and set to washing dishes. When Lori tried to shoo him away, he just shook his head and, speaking louder than she ever remembered him doing, told her that dishes were his job and had been his job for as long as The Diner had been there. A glance at her boss, shrugging her shoulders, and Lori smiled, thanked the man, wished him Merry Christmas, and pushed back through the door to the dining area.

She sat down with Marcus and Michah and was silent for a while. "Everything okay, Lori?" Marcus asked, seeing a faraway look in her eyes.

Pulling herself back to the present, she nodded. "Yes. Fine. Mr. Tam just insists on doing the dishes."

Reaching into the bag at her feet, she pulled out the two packages. "I got you guys presents. They aren't much, but . . . Christmas isn't the same to me if I can't give someone something." Quickly she swiped at a tear that started a path down her cheek. Turning away, she hoped no one saw.

"We got you something too," Marcus said, trying hard to pretend he didn't see her hiding her tears. He really hoped she would open up soon and tell him the rest of her story.

"But you gave me the little tree; you shouldn't have bought anything else." She spoke softly, her voice shaking.

"Lori? Do you need to stay here and help? The crowd has thinned out a lot," Michah said, glancing from her to his brother.

"No. No, I didn't have to come at all, but I wanted to. I wanted to spend the day with the only friends I have anymore." Marcus heard a barely audible "My family" tacked on the end of that.

"Let's take our presents back to our apartment. We can have hot cocoa while we open them," Michah suggested as Lori stood and Marcus took her arm. They looked around the room and said a quick "Good night and Merry Christmas" to everyone before they walked out into the fading sun of the late afternoon.

Once they arrived at the small apartment, Michah made himself scarce in the tiny galley kitchen heating water for the hot cocoa. He found a bag of small marshmallows and put a peppermint stick in each mug. He could hear Marcus speaking softly to Lori on the other side of the thin wall. She was sobbing.

"Lori, please talk to me. Tell me what's wrong. I will do everything in my power to help you fix it," Marcus begged.

"I'm sorry," Lori sobbed. "I just miss my family so much . . ." She trailed off.

"Here." Marcus handed her the small wrapped package. "Open your present. I think it may help you feel better."

Lori eyed him strangely as she took the gift. Michah moved into the room and set the cocoa on the crate they used to store books and as a coffee table. Brushing tears from her cheeks, Lori pulled at the tape holding the paper around the package.

"A phone." She spoke in a quivering voice. "You gave me a phone?" She looked first at Michah and then Marcus, a question in her eyes.

"I wanted to be able to talk to you even when I can't see you," Marcus told her. "And we both wanted to do something to help you feel safer and help you talk to your family and friends back East." He added.

Lori burst into tears again. "I appreciate the thought." she got out. "And I will feel safer," she added. "But I can't talk to my family."

When she broke down and sobbed again, Marcus couldn't take it anymore. He pulled her into his arms and held her close and tight. "Please, Lori. Help me understand what's going on," he begged.

Michah sat nearby, head bowed, silently praying.

Lori shook her head. "It's too long a story." She tried to make excuses for keeping her past to herself. "You won't believe it anyhow."

"Try us," Michah challenged.

"It's weighing you down, sweetheart." Marcus spoke gently. "You need to share that burden. Lighten that load."

He called me sweetheart? Lori thought to herself and could only hold on to that. *Curtis called me sweetheart too. Then he broke my heart.* Shuddering, she pulled away from Marcus's arms and immediately felt bereft of his warmth, his strength.

"Lori?" Michah spoke gently. "God created our friendship. You've got to know that." He struggled for words to encourage, not frighten, her. He had seen the fear in her eyes when she pulled away from Marcus. Reading his twin like a book, he knew Marcus was trying to figure out the same thing he was: Why did a term of endearment terrify her?

Taking a deep breath, Lori tried to speak. Words filled her mouth, but it was hard to get them out. She couldn't bear to have the twins, her dearest friends, walk away. Hot tears continued their tracks down her cheeks. Swiping at them and shuddering a breath, she finally found her voice.

"I can't call my family because the man I'm hiding from might find me. He might have a trace on their phone." If possible, she cried harder. "For all I know, he's terrorizing them in the hopes they will break and tell him where I am. They don't know where I am, and I can't tell them where I am."

Marcus reached out to her but didn't touch her. Lori stared at his open arms a moment before she leaned into them and allowed him to wrap her in his warmth. She felt safe there somehow.

The room was silent, save for the click of the radiators. The cocoa sat cooling, untouched on the crate. Marcus and Michah exchanged silent, telling looks over the top of Lori's head. Lori, who had wound her way into both their hearts, continued to silently cry. Marcus's shirt was wet with her tears.

She could not let go. She clung to Marcus like a drowning woman clings to a life preserver. The need to tell them everything surged inside her. Her heart insisted. Her head screamed, *"No!"* Finally her heart won. It convinced her head that if Curtis had found her, Marcus and Michah would only be safe if they stayed away from her. She needed them to want to go away.

"I was seriously involved with a man named Curtis before I moved here," she began. "He was everything I thought I wanted. He was a perfect gentleman. He was handsome. And he always had money to do fun things together. He told me he loved me. He hinted at marriage." Stopping briefly, she gathered her thoughts again as she sipped her cocoa.

"The only thing that ever bothered me was that he always had an excuse not to go to church with me." She shook her head. "I let it go because I believed all of it was important. It was part of his job. And I really wasn't happy with the church I was raised in anyhow. If I had never gone there before, I wouldn't have wanted to go there. I even started missing Sundays occasionally to do something fun with him. It didn't feel right, but it didn't feel wrong, either." Lori shrugged her shoulders. "I finally made up my mind to find a different church—one that Curtis would enjoy going to, one we could go to together."

Heaving a sigh, she continued. "My brother, Todd, is a detective on the local police force. He'd just gotten the promotion a few days before I met Curtis." She snorted. "I've since then come to wonder if he arranged to meet me so he could keep tabs on Todd. I haven't figured out the why of it, though. Maybe their paths crossed somewhere? Todd didn't know Curtis until I introduced them, though, so . . ." She trailed off.

Then, taking a deep breath, she continued. "On occasion, Curtis would ask me to pick him up somewhere and then we could go directly to the restaurant or the theater or wherever." She waved her hand dismissively. "I always did. It made sense. I never once questioned it."

After a pause and another sip of cocoa, she went on to say, "Then, one day at lunch, he asked me if I could pick him up at midnight that night and take him to the airport. He didn't want to leave his car parked there for the week he planned to be away." Shrugging, she continued. "I told him I would. I didn't even think to question why he was flying out at midnight. I didn't talk to him anymore that day because he said he would be in meetings till late."

Lori never raised her eyes, never looked at Marcus or Michah as she told the story. Her cheeks flamed red with the heat of her shame and embarrassment.

"He sent me a text a little after six and told me there was a slight change of plans. I was not to pick him up at his apartment at midnight. I needed to go there earlier and retrieve his luggage and take it with me to pick him up at the bank at midnight. The meetings were running a lot later than expected.

"He had given me a key to his apartment during lunch so I could take his mail in while he was gone," she remembered. "I didn't even think to wonder if he had planned on having me pick up his luggage all along. At least, not then."

Lori had long since pushed from Marcus's embrace and was sitting up ramrod straight. Now her fists were clenched so tightly her knuckles turned white. Her face was still red, but it was anger now instead of embarrassment. "Todd was home when I got the text. I jokingly said something to him about how I hoped the robbery ring didn't hit that bank that night and accidentally hop in my car to get away instead of their own."

Looking Marcus in the eye, she continued. "Todd didn't even crack a smile. He sat down on the couch beside me and started grilling me like I was a common criminal. Come to find out, I almost was. Curtis wanted me to drive the getaway car and take him and his cohorts to the airport. I'm pretty sure my body would have been found in my car somewhere. No loose ends that way," she continued matter-of-factly.

"I was on my way to a private airstrip by 8:00 and on my way to Atlanta, Georgia, by 8:30. A female officer was in my car, with my phone, in the back parking lot of the bank shortly before midnight." Shaking her head in frustration, Lori added, "He was so sure of me, he just knew I would be there."

Blowing out a breath, she finished the story. "One of the robbers was shot trying to escape. I read in the news he died later in the hospital. One of them was caught, and I think he's had his trial and gone to prison. And the night watchman was shot and died during surgery.

"My brother, Todd, told me the one time we've spoken since I left that Curtis's real name is Charles Arnold. I called Todd the very next morning while I was in Memphis. The plan had been for me to be able to go back home if the man was captured. But because he got away, I had to keep running. And since then the only information I've been able to get has been from the bits and pieces on television or in the papers people leave at The Diner." Bowing her head, she continued quietly, "Curtis got away. As far as I know, he's never been caught."

Standing up, Lori walked toward the door, grabbing her coat from the rack beside it. "I'll see myself out now." She put her hand on the knob.

"Lori! No! Please stay!" Both men were talking at once, and she was too befuddled to know who said what. The thing that did come across clearly was that neither of them wanted her to leave.

"If Curtis has found me, I could put you both in danger." Shaking her head and opening the door, she added, "I care too much for both of you to ever do that. I need to go. Now." She walked out the door.

Marcus and Michah rose as one and plowed to the door, Marcus flinging it open and nearly knocking his brother down shoving through it. Michah slammed it shut behind him and then thought to wonder if Marcus had the key. He knew he didn't.

They caught up with Lori before she reached the building's exit door. Each grabbing an arm, they brought her to a halt. "Lori, if you're in danger, you should not be walking around by yourself at night," Marcus stated. "We can't let you do that."

"I'm afraid you're stuck with us, sister!" Michah grinned as they turned her around to march her back to their apartment. "We will help you. We care too much to ever even think of letting you do this alone."

"Do you think Curtis has found you?" Marcus asked, using the name Lori was most familiar with after they had gotten back inside their apartment, which, fortunately, they hadn't been locked out of. "And why do you think he may have found you?" he wanted to know.

Shrugging out of her coat and settling back into her seat on the sofa, Lori breathed a sigh of relief and lifted up a grateful prayer before attempting to answer him. "I don't know anything. I just feel like someone is watching me sometimes. You've heard people say things like how the hair on the back of their neck stands up, right?" Both men nodded. "Well, the hair on the back of my neck stands up," she stated simply.

"Okay." Michah cleared his throat. "Here's what we're going to do."

Marcus and Lori listened as Michah told them of a plan that was forming in his mind to contact Lori's brother, Todd, in Pittsburgh while he, Michah, was at the Missions headquarters in Florida in January.

"I promise you, I will make sure your brother, Todd, is the only one who hears about where you are. I can, and I will, do this. Everything will be okay. I promise," Michah stated.

Marcus nodded as he looked from Michah to Lori. She didn't look at all sure of Michah's promise. "I don't think you understand," she told Michah. "Curtis has friends, snitches, everywhere. They could easily listen in on any conversation you have with Todd." Shaking her head, she added. "No. No, thank you. It's too risky. No one back home can know anything about where I am or what I'm doing. Curtis will find out, and I would have to find someplace else to go." She didn't add that she didn't have enough money to go anywhere.

Taking another sip of the cocoa Michah had reheated for them, she pasted on a smile and said, "Open your presents, guys!" Then, somewhat embarrassed, she added, "They are nowhere near as nice as what you've given me, but I'm hoping you like them."

Marcus and Michah ripped open the small packages and simultaneously grinned and chuckled. Lori was happy to know they really did like her gifts for them. Marcus even kept them all laughing reading jokes from his pulpit humor book.

The Boys drove Lori home around nine, and both walked with her up to her apartment. They had plugged their numbers into her new cell phone, and she had to admit she did feel safer having it. And lighter. She felt lighter having shared her troubles with Marcus and Michah.

Marcus had walked into her rooms ahead of her while Michah stood guard in the hallway. After a quick but careful look around to make sure no one was there, Marcus brushed a kiss across her cheek and told her to lock up behind him. "I will," she promised. "And thank you again. For everything." Smiling, she added, "The phone does make me feel safer. And sharing has eased the burden. A lot."

Stretching up on her tiptoes, she touched her lips to his. Electricity flowed through her. The way Marcus's eyes widened, she was sure he felt it too. Clearing his throat, he stepped through the door to join his brother. "Merry Christmas, Lori. I'll talk to you tomorrow," he said simply. Then, with a smile and a wink, he trailed Michah down the hall.

Lori locked the door and pressed her forehead to the solid surface of it. Her fingers pressed to her lips, she questioned herself. *Why did I do that? I really need to stop flirting with him. I'm only going to get in his way.*

Knowing she was a long way from sleep, she curled up on her sofa and found herself fixated on that electrical current. What was that about, anyhow? She had heard people talk about sparks flying when you find true love, but she had never really believed it to be true—literally or otherwise.

Marcus's face appeared in her mind's eye: his dark brown hair, cropped short but still trying to fling itself into curls; those deep brown eyes that she wanted to fall into. They mesmerized her. Long, dark lashes that Lori knew some women would kill for. And that adorable dimple when he smiled at her.

Her head jerked up when it hit her. She was in love with Marcus. She knew she felt safer with him than she ever had with any other man, even her brother the detective. She had certainly never felt this safe with Curtis. Come to think of it, she had never really felt anything with Curtis—just that she was having fun and, perhaps, fulfilling some duty by finding a man to marry and raise a family with.

And why did that feel like a duty? No one had ever told her she had to do that. But everyone she knew was getting married. It dawned on her that she had missed her best friend's wedding last week. She had forgotten all about it. She was supposed to be the maid of honor.

Briefly she wondered if Todd was still dating the same girl he was seeing when she left. And did he give her a ring for Christmas? Would she miss her own brother's wedding too?

And Michah's wild idea to call her family for her and tell them she was safe and she had friends. She really hoped he understood he could not do that. Even though she wasn't actually in a witness protection program, what her brother did—sending her away, having her sever all contact with her friends and family—was certainly close. She had not been given a new identity. That was about the only difference. Maybe she should have told Todd to get that for her. Maybe she should be in witness protection.

At the time, her little jaunt off into the unknown had been nothing more than a quick, temporary fix to put her out of harm's way for the immediate future. Everyone expected the ring to be broken up that night. Everyone expected Curtis to be captured and sent to jail like his cohort had been. And really they were just guessing that this was the robbery ring when he put her on Chuck's plane, and she was already long gone by the time they knew they had guessed correctly.

The night she disappeared, she had found herself wondering more than once, *What if Todd was wrong?* His gut was never wrong, though.

And now here she was, three months later, still stuck being Lori Wright and living someone else's life. It was starting to feel like this was her life. For the rest of her life. No one had ever asked, but she thought often about the business degree she would have had within a few months. Had anyone ever wondered what plans for the future Lori had sacrificed when she became a waitress and a maid? She would never be an accountant. Never run a business. Never help people with their taxes.

Actually, all of that sounded rather dull to her now. The work she was doing was fun, especially the waitressing. She really enjoyed that job. And when had that happened?

She had never waited tables until she came to Tulsa. Finding she enjoyed it felt strange.

CHAPTER SIX

———†———

L ori kissed him! He had certainly not expected that. He hadn't expected a lot of what had happened today. He was still lit up from that electrical spark that jolted him when her lips touched his. The touch was brief, but it was powerful. It shook him and nearly brought him to his knees.

And then he winked at her? Whatever was that about? Why on earth did he do something silly like that? He could have kissed her back. He could have shown her how much he cared for her. But he winked. Sighing, he flopped over on his other side in bed. Sleep was very illusive tonight. It had been such a strange day. A good day, he had to admit, remembering that kiss. He rolled over again.

"You can't sleep either, bro?" Michah asked from his bed on the other side of the room. "Feel like talking?"

"Yeah, I do. I just don't know what to say or where to begin," Marcus admitted.

"You love her, Marcus." It wasn't a question. Michah knew his twin too well to need to ask.

"I don't even know when I fell for her," he sighed. "It's almost like it was always there—even before I met her." In the dark, he shook his head. Michah would know without seeing the movement.

"The very first moment I laid eyes on her, I knew she was the one for you, big brother." Michah spoke softly, almost reverently. "God chose her for you."

"I know," Marcus whispered and felt a tear trail down his cheek. "I fear for her. Those rooms aren't safe even if Curtis isn't here. It isn't safe for her to walk everywhere, especially after dark." On a sigh, he added, "I just wish there was something I could do to help her."

"There's something I can do," Michah told him.

"No, bro. She said it wasn't safe to contact her family." Marcus sat up and put his feet on the floor. "Please don't call them."

"I won't. Not from here. And not from my phone." Michah reminded his brother that he was going to Florida in January to train with a missions organization down there. "Near the end of the two weeks I'm there I'm going to buy a burner phone and call the police station her brother works at. I won't tell him who I am. I won't tell him where I live or where Lori lives. I'm only going to tell him she's okay and she has friends looking out for her. And I'll see if there are any messages for her. Then I'll throw the phone away."

"Florida is a long way from Oklahoma," Marcus said thoughtfully. "It could work. Just be very careful, Michah. You cannot give anything away. I won't take any chances on you putting Lori in danger!"

"Relax. I love you and my future sister-in-law way too much to ever put her in danger," Michah promised.

It had been a long time since Matt had climbed a tree, but the boss was paying him good money to do it, so up he went. He had to be careful of that bottle in his pocket. He couldn't afford to have it get broken. Not yet, anyhow.

Lori woke with a start. When she tried to turn her head, pain radiated from her neck up into her head and down to her shoulders. Raising her arms, she massaged the tight, achy, muscles. "That's what I get for passing out on the couch," she groaned to herself.

As she reached over to turn on the lamp, she heard a noise that sounded like something sliding coming from her bedroom. Picking up her boots and her coat from where she'd dropped them by the sofa, she walked in socked feet toward the bedroom door.

Something thudded in the bedroom, and she realized the sliding noise she had heard was her window being raised. Near panic, heart pounding loudly in her ears, she hurried to the apartment's entry door and, opening the door, stepped on silent feet into the hallway, quietly closing it behind her.

Someone was in her bedroom. Was it Curtis Maquire? She wasn't going to stick around to find out. Hurrying down the stairs in stocking feet, she stopped only a moment to slip her feet into her boots before opening the door and dashing across the porch and out onto the sidewalk, putting her coat on as she flew. Two blocks later, she slipped between two houses that she knew were empty and dashed into the backyard. Pushed deep into the shadows of a storage shed behind one of the houses, she put her hands in her coat pockets and stood shivering, wondering what to do next. Realizing she was gripping her new phone, she pulled it out of her pocket and called 911.

"What is your emergency?" the operator asked loudly. Too loudly.

"Someone just broke into my apartment," Lori whispered, and then, still whispering, she gave the woman her address.

When the operator spoke again, her voice was much softer. She understood Lori was in hiding. "A unit is on the way now. What is your location?" Lori gave her address again. "No, ma'am, where are you at right now? Are you still in the apartment?" she wanted to know.

"Oh. No, I was on the sofa in the living area when he raised the bedroom window. I ran out the door and didn't stop until I was two blocks away." She told her where she was hiding.

"Stay put, and I will send another unit to pick you up," the woman told her. "Please stay on the line with me till they find you."

"Okay. Thank you." Lori thought briefly of what kind of conversation she could have with the operator while she waited to be picked up. Then she realized that even though the line was still open, the woman had taken another call and was sending out a fire truck.

Hearing sirens in the distance and coming closer prompted Lori to ask, "I thought you would send them in silent. Why do I hear sirens?"

"Ma'am, that's the fire department. The police called in a fire as they were en route to your address." The woman spoke briefly with someone and then spoke to Lori again. "There is a unit on the street at the location you gave me earlier. You are still hiding behind the vacant houses?" she wanted to know.

"Yes, yes, I am. And I see police lights flashing between the two houses. I'm going to walk up between them to the street."

"I'll stay right here on the line with you," the woman assured her.

Peeking out between the houses, Lori saw the cruiser parked on the street directly in front of her. Breathing a sigh of relief, she walked between the houses and up to the street, where two officers stood near their car, hands hovering near their weapons, heads turning, on full alert.

"Officers?" Her voice shook. They turned as one when they heard her. "Thank you for finding me." Then, into the phone, she said "Thank you for staying on the line with me. I'm with the officers now." She tapped the phone to hang up.

The officer nearest her opened the back door of the cruiser and helped her in. "I'm Officer Ryan," he said by way of introduction. "That's my partner, Officer James," he said, nodding toward the man getting behind the wheel.

Officer James mumbled a "How do?" before shifting into drive, checking his mirrors, and heading back down the street toward Lori's rooms.

Lori quickly realized it was her home that was on fire. "No. No, it can't be!" As soon as the car stopped, she tried to open her door, then realized it was locked on the inside because it was used to transport prisoners.

"Officer Ryan!" she called to him. When he glanced back at her, she said, "Please, let me out! My home is on fire!"

"I'm sorry, ma'am; I can't do that. You're safer where you are." And with that he hurried away.

Lori jammed her hands in her pockets, frustrated. When she realized she was gripping her phone again, her Christmas gift from the Boys, she pulled it out and tapped Marcus's number. He answered on the second ring.

"Lori? What's going on? Are you okay?" Glancing at the clock, Marcus realized it was 2:00 in the morning. Swinging his feet out of bed, he saw his twin getting up and reaching for his jeans. We're on our way, honey. The officer is right; you should stay put. You are safer in the car." He fumbled with his clothes as he dressed. Michah thought to give him a hand with his shirt and boots. Palming the keys, he twin-talked to Marcus that he was going for the car and would meet him at the front door.

Marcus switched hands and held the phone with his shoulder. Contorting himself in more ways than he ever knew he could, he got dressed and headed out the door, speaking calmly to Lori the whole time.

Michah drove the several blocks to Lori's apartment while Marcus continued to talk to her—or mostly listen. "Curtis must have found me," she whimpered. "Who else would break into any apartment in that old house? No one who lives there has anything worth stealing. And the fire—he must have started it to kill me."

"Was there a fire while you were in there?" Marcus asked. "'Cause I'm not sure the fire was meant to kill you," he continued. "He had to have lit it as a warning, Lori. He just wanted to frighten you." While that wasn't going to make her feel better, at least it would help her see the situation a little more clearly for what it was: a scare tactic meant to keep Lori silent.

Marcus really hoped he was right, that this was just a scare tactic. He didn't want to think anyone would want to kill someone. He didn't want to think anyone would want to kill Lori.

"You're right," she agreed. "And he succeeded. I am officially terrified!"

Two hours later, the men waited near the reception desk at the police station while Lori gave her statement in one of the offices down the hall.

"I was gone most of the day," Lori explained for what seemed like the hundredth time. "The Diner had a big Christmas dinner this year for all of the employees and their guests, the regulars, and any homeless folks who showed up. I believe they do it every year."

"Yes, we know about Tonya's philanthropic efforts," Detective Stewart Mitchell told her. "What time did you leave there?"

"Sometime around four. A little after, I think. I went with my friends to their apartment and hung out with them until they brought me home around nine." Shrugging her shoulders, she continued, "I fell asleep on my sofa and I woke up when someone opened my bedroom window. The thing never has latched properly. I told my landlord, but since I'm on the second floor, I guess it wasn't very important."

"Were you burning any candles?" Lori shook her head. "Do you smoke?"

"No!" Panic shot through her. Did they think she burned the building down? It wasn't a total loss. At least she didn't think so. "Please, tell me, do I have a home to go back to?"

Someone tapped on the door and the detective walked over and pulled it open. Stepping into the hallway, he closed the door behind him. Lori could hear them talking but couldn't understand what was being said. She was so tired it took more effort than she had the energy for to wipe the tears that tracked down her face. Shivering, she pulled her coat tighter around her as the door pushed open and the detective came back into the room.

"Do you have any enemies?" The blunt question took her by surprise. She tried to breathe, tried to speak, but her body was frozen with fear. She nodded. The man took the chair across from her. She saw something different in his eyes now. They seemed softer than they were a few minutes ago. Was it sympathy?

"Someone did purposely start the fire." Inhaling and exhaling deeply, the detective scrubbed a hand across his face before he spoke again. "Who's your enemy, Lori?" She saw for the first time the dark circles under his eyes. He was exhausted too.

"Curtis Maquire . . . er, Charles Arnold," she corrected herself, "from Pittsburgh, Pennsylvania." As she told him the story, she realized it was the second time in less than twelve hours that she had told it. Did telling Marcus and Michah make it easier this time?

For the most part, Marcus and Michah sat in silence, engrossed in their own thoughts. Remembering all the trials they had faced growing up. Remembering the people who had reached out to them, brought them to where they were today.

"I had a dream about Pastor Carlton." Marcus spoke out of the blue. "I was dreaming when my phone rang."

Michah faced his brother. Memories of the past, their past, flooded him and threatened to drown out everything here, everything now. "Tell me," was all he said.

"We were back at the old church, the one the flood destroyed." Marcus spoke, both boys flashing through memories of the old country church their parents had taken them to as small children. The church had been destroyed by a huge flood when they were nine years old.

Shaking his head, Michah spoke. "I hadn't thought about that place in a long time. But what could Pastor Carlton possibly have to do with that place?" he asked.

Long moments of silence passed between them as they each remembered their horrors from the past and their victories through the blessings God had provided in the form of a true Christian that had interceded and opened up the path they were on now.

Finally, Marcus spoke. "He just said 'The past is the past, and it needs to stay there.' Then my phone rang."

"Lori's past," Michah said.

"Our past too," Marcus corrected. "Our past is every bit as sordid as hers, little brother."

The little country church the Stout family had attended had a preacher who did everything but live the gospel he preached. The boys had thought of him as the devil himself when they were growing up. The adults at the church didn't seem to have a clue what was really happening there. The flood had revealed it all.

The preacher and his wife and sons had left town for a week and expected to return on Saturday. Between Tuesday evening and Friday morning, the area had gotten almost ten inches of rain, overflowing the creek that normally babbled peacefully by the church.

Late Saturday morning some of the men from the church had gone over to check on things, only to find the entire basement underwater. Among the Bibles, hymn books, and children's crayon drawings of Jesus and His sheep floating around in the basement were soggy pictures of the children in the preacher's Tuesday evening Bible class—naked children. The preacher went to jail. His family was broken. The church saw the business end of a bulldozer.

Marcus, Michah, and a dozen other children went to counseling to help them understand the wrong that had been done to them and that none of it was their fault. Some of the children—the girls, especially—still struggled, the twins knew. One of the boys was in prison himself for following in that preacher's footsteps.

The Stout family had struggled with the aftermath for almost two years until one of the other affected families had convinced them to go to Pastor Carlton's church. It was their saving grace.

Reading his twin's thoughts, Marcus spoke. "Pastor Carlton was always there for us, our whole family. Anytime and every time we needed him." Memories of his fear of being alone with any man other than his father still had the power to shake him.

"His first thought was always of our comfort and feeling safe," Michah remembered out loud. "He took us all under his wing and restored our faith in man by letting us choose how much faith we had in him."

"It was never really about faith in him, though," Marcus added. "He ultimately restored our faith in Christ so we could begin to trust men again."

Michah nodded agreement. "Did he say anything else?" Michah wanted to know. Marcus just shook his head.

Eventually Lori was allowed to leave. A phone call to her boss assured her she had the whole day to sort out her future. "Honey, you aren't due here till four," Tonya reminded her. "And if that isn't enough time, just let me know by two and I'll get your shift covered for you," her boss told her, compassion threading through her voice.

"Where are you going to stay till you can get back into your home?" she wanted to know.

Lori was so overwhelmed by the events of the night that she hadn't really stopped to consider that.

Her hesitation to answer must have been her tell, because her boss spoke again to tell her, "Come to my house. I have an empty bedroom. You are more than welcome to use it till you can get back into your own place, wherever that ends up being."

"Oh! I couldn't impose on . . ." Lori began.

"Nonsense! You would not be imposing." Shaking her head and chuckling softly, she continued, "You have become one of my most trusted and reliable employees, Lori. The customers adore you. And if it's not enough that I want you safe and cared for, maybe you should consider that they want that for you too."

Left nearly speechless by her boss's thoughtfulness and caring, she was barely audible when she responded with a soft and shaky "Thank you."

Lori put Michah on the phone to take her boss's information. They would drive her over there after a quick stop at Lori's rooms to see if she could retrieve anything and then a stop at The Diner for a key. Michah had spoken to an officer who he knew through his dispatch position, and the officer had assured him that even though the old house was not a total loss, it probably wasn't worth repairing, and Lori's rooms were at the heart of the fire. There would be nothing left.

When they pulled up in front of the old rooming house, the tears Lori thought she was surely out of slid down her cheeks and splashed softly onto her coat. Swiping at them, she got out of the car and stood for a moment, trying to digest the scene in front of her. She was conscious of the twins coming up to stand protectively, one on each side of her. One grasped each elbow as though they feared she would collapse if they didn't. Perhaps she would.

Shaky legs carried her up to the yellow police tape that surrounded the building. Marcus's strong arm wound around her waist and pulled her against the length of him. She accepted his quiet strength without a second thought. Michah still held her elbow on the other side and stood close, brushing against her as well. She felt protected. More than that, she felt cherished.

An officer approached and, recognizing Michah, spoke to him. "Michah. This is a crime scene, buddy. No one can cross the tape."

Michah nodded and answered the man politely. "Yes, sir, we understand. Lori here"—he tilted his head toward her—"lives here. Lived here. We came by to see if there was anything left from her rooms that she could claim."

Eyeing her gently, understanding now who she was, the officer spoke to her. "Ma'am, I'm truly sorry. Your apartment is where the incendiary device was found. There is nothing left." Tipping his hat, he hurried off in response to a shout from a suited man at the rear of the building.

"I don't even have my purse anymore," Lori whimpered and collapsed against Marcus. His strong arms held and supported her as they returned to the car.

CHAPTER SEVEN

———————†———————

At The Diner, Lori pushed the food around on her plate, lost in thought and unaware of the whispering around her. She felt, rather than saw, one of the other waitresses standing beside her.

"Lori, honey, we've been taking up a collection all morning. It's not much, but you can maybe get a few clothes and toiletries."

Aware for the first time that she was still in the clothes she had put on yesterday morning—Christmas morning—she jumped up, knocking over her chair, and fled to the women's restroom. Washing her face, staring at herself in the mirror, embarrassment threatened to overwhelm her. Her eyes were red from crying. Dark circles told the story of her lack of sleep. Her long, blond hair was stringy and tangled. She washed her face and worked her fingers through her hair.

Her boss quietly entered the room and stood behind her. Their eyes met in the mirror. She pulled Lori's hair back, behind her shoulders, and gently tugged and tidied it with her fingers. Retrieving an elastic band from deep inside one of her apron pockets, she pulled it into a messy ponytail. Nothing was said, but there was understanding. Pressing a key into Lori's hand, she pushed back through the door.

Taking a deep breath, Lori walked back into the dining room. The waitress still hovered near the table where Marcus and Michah still sat, all the chairs upright and in place. She handed Lori a fat envelope and pulled her in for a hug. "We love you, Lori. And we're all glad you're okay." Tears shimmered in her eyes as more threatened to spill down Lori's cheeks. "Go, buy what you need, get some rest, and come back to us as soon as you're up for it." Then she added, for Lori's ears only, "I'll cover for you if you aren't up for your shift tonight."

Feeling overwhelmed and speechless, Lori hugged the girl back, accepting the envelope. "I'll pay you back," she managed to croak.

"Oh, honey, no," the waitress began. "You can't pay it back. No one knows who gave what." Smiling through the tears that ran down her cheeks, she clasped Lori's hand briefly and turned toward the kitchen to pick up an order.

Lori stood still, staring into space, lost in thought. Exhaustion etched fine lines in her features and the dark circles under her eyes attested to just how worn she was. A strong hand took her arm. "Come on, Lori. Let's get you out of here." Marcus spoke against her ear. She let him lead her through the door.

It was already after nine and all the stores were open for business. Their first stop was the resale shop nearby. Lori was able to find two pairs of decent jeans, a purse, and three sweaters. She also chose a pair of sweatpants and a sweatshirt, good enough to sleep in. A trip to the big box store near the interstate got her some sneakers, underclothes, socks, and basic toiletries.

Back in the car and headed to her boss's house, she counted out what was left in the envelope. "I still have $16.89," she said aloud, thinking to herself that it was more than she had in the purse that the fire had burned up.

The Boys carried her purchases, and very nearly carried her too, into the house her boss lived in. It was small, just two bedrooms and one bath, but tidy and comfortable. The furniture was old and a little worn but sturdy.

"Let me get this thrift store stuff into the washer for you, honey," Marcus suggested. "You can take a long, hot shower and get it into the dryer before you get some sleep."

Lori nodded absently as Marcus found the laundry area behind a set of large bifold doors and got the washer started. "As soon as this gets started, we're out of here. The key is on the bedside table in the spare room. Your phone has an alarm app to wake you up in time to get ready for your shift," he told her. Then he added, "I'm sure no one will fault you if you miss work tonight. We will stay if you want us to." He looked into the depths of those fear-filled eyes—green eyes that held him captive.

"No . . . no, thank you." She shook her head. "You've done so much already. I'll be fine. I'm sure." Sighing deeply, she said, "I just want a long, hot shower and a comfortable bed right now."

Michah hugged her and Marcus held her close a bit longer than he probably should have and kissed the top of her head before letting her go. "Lock the door behind us. And call if you need anything at all," he told her as he brushed her hair back from her cheek, tucking it behind her ear.

"Call us when you've rested. If you decide to go to work, we will come and give you a ride," Michah told her. "Honestly, a night off would be a good thing for you," he added.

Nodding, Lori shut the door and turned the deadbolt. She leaned against the door for a moment as the last twelve hours replayed through her mind like a bad VCR tape. Thoughts skipped and jumped around. The scary ones stuck and played themselves over and over again. Numb, she walked down the hall to the bathroom and stood under the hot, steamy water for a long time.

Her body felt better when she toweled off, but her mind was still stuck on that replay loop. After transferring her clothes to the dryer, she crawled between the sheets of the most comfortable bed she had ever slept in. And she did sleep. Soundly.

Music from an unfamiliar song woke her. After a moment, she realized her phone was ringing. It was Marcus. "Hello." She spoke through a haze of sleep.

"You were sleeping. Honey, I'm sorry. I shouldn't have woken you up," Marcus apologized.

"It's okay," she told him quickly, sitting up and remembering where she was. "What time is it?"

"Almost 3:00." He spoke casually. "Please tell me you are going to stay home and rest tonight," he said.

It slammed her, nearly took her breath away. It was almost 3:00! And she had no home! "Oh! Oh dear!" She pushed out of the bed and stood, looking around, trying to find clothes, and then she remembered they were still in the drier. "No. No, I'm going to work. Can you please pick me up in about a half hour?" She hung up the phone and hurried to the laundry room to retrieve her laundry.

After quickly dressing and dealing with her hair, she brushed her teeth and cleaned up after herself. She could not, would not, leave her boss's home in a shamble.

The Boys arrived at 3:30 on the dot and they headed toward The Diner. Michah was clocking in at four also, and Marcus had until six. He had decided to run a few errands while he had the car out and a little time on his hands. "Do you by any chance still have the phone charger?" he asked Lori.

Looking momentarily bewildered, she finally shook her head. "It was still in my purse. I'm sorry."

"I'll pick up another while I'm out running errands," he told her. Grinning, he added, "I'll pick up an alarm clock too."

Looking sheepishly out the side window, Lori thanked him and opened her purse. "Do you think fifteen dollars will cover it?" she wanted to know.

"Put your money away. I've got this." He caught her eyes in the rearview mirror.

"Then I should at least give you gas money . . ." She trailed off as both men stared her down.

"We've got this, Lori. We've got this." Michah's voice was firm and compassionate.

Giving up, she closed her purse and sat back in the seat, trying to relax. "Thank you," she said, and then chuckled. "I seem to be saying that a lot lately." She shook her head. "It doesn't seem like nearly enough, though."

"It's all that's necessary. More than enough," Marcus told her, catching her eye in the rearview again.

Lori was surprised to find herself the recipient of another envelope of cash that customers and lunch shift employees had stuffed for her. "I don't know what to say" was all she could manage when Mr. Tam handed it to her. "I'm overwhelmed with all your kindness and . . ." she trailed off, brushing an escaping tear from her cheek. "Thank you so much."

Mr. Tam put a bony arm around her shoulders for a brief side hug. "You're a good person, Lori. And a great waitress." Smiling, he patted her shoulder before removing his arm. "We all care. And you're welcome," he added before he shuffled off to his usual table and took a seat, turning his cup upright in a silent request for coffee. Lori quickly retrieved the pot and obliged.

A little after midnight, Michah arrived to take Lori to her boss's house. He would pick her up the next day around 3:30 to take her back to The Diner. For this week at least, their schedules coincided conveniently that way.

The next afternoon on the way to The Diner, Michah let her know, "Marcus told me to tell you he would take you to get your new driver's license and Social Security card and whatever else you need to replace from your purse."

"Oh. Okay," she responded, sounding a bit distracted.

Michah took a long look at her while they sat at a red light. She looked more than a little out of sorts. She looked exhausted. "You okay, Lori?" he asked gently.

She barely nodded a response.

"Talk to me?" It was a question and it was filled with concern. "What's going on?" Michah glanced her way again.

Heaving a breath, she answered, "Since I don't have a car, I don't really need a license, so no need to get it replaced. And how often will I need my Social Security card? I really don't need to get them replaced." Shrugging her shoulders, she added, "I don't even have an address for them." Refusing to look at Michah, she stared out the passenger window instead.

"Okay," he responded simply, realizing that maybe this was more about her lack of money. And she was right about her need for an address.

"So how long do you think it will be till you're ready to look for an apartment again?" He tried changing the subject.

Their arrival at The Diner gave Lori an excuse not to answer. "Thank you for the ride, Michah. I'll see you later!" she said a little too cheerily as she escaped from the car and ran inside.

Checking his mirrors and pulling from the curb, Michah thought he understood what was happening. Lori was going to run again. Marcus would be heartbroken when she did.

The longer she stayed in one place, the greater the chances of Curtis getting to her. Lori knew she was in danger. Anyone she was near was in danger. Michah had asked a great question. When would she start looking for another apartment? More specifically: When would she look for a new place to run to?

CHAPTER EIGHT

———————†———————

"Boss, we scraped some blood and skin off the tree outside Ms. Wright's window. Forensics is running it now looking for a DNA match," the young officer told Detective Mitchell.

This case was bigger, more convoluted, than anything Mitchell had seen in a while. Even though nothing seemed to fit together, his gut told him everything did go together. They were dealing with one criminal. Well, maybe more than one person but all of them set on accomplishing the same crimes.

The conversation he had with Ms. Wright's brother, Detective Todd Wright, back in Pittsburgh had been enlightening, to say the least. Charles Arnold, aka Curtis Maquire, was trouble—maybe more than Mitchell had ever dealt with before.

The Pittsburgh detective had filled him in on what had happened to Lori. The two had talked at length about the robberies in Boston and Pittsburgh. Mitchell wondered to himself about a bank robbery that had happened two weeks ago in Tulsa. He mentioned it to Wright, and that detective jumped on it. Mitchell gave him as many details as he had—and there weren't many. These thieves were pros.

"What kind of safe was it?" Todd wanted to know.

"Old," Mitchell told him. "They got it open using the combination. The safe wasn't damaged at all, but it sure was empty."

"That's our crew," Wright told him. "We think they use a stethoscope and listen for the clicks."

"That sure narrows down the number of banks they can hit." Mitchell spoke thoughtfully. "I'll get my guys out there locating which banks they'll be interested in."

"Simpson's an idiot!" Conrad Meyer grumbled to himself. "One simple direction and he blew it. Lori was supposed to be *in* her apartment—if you could call that hole in the wall an apartment."

He knew the real problem was Simpson's lack of motivation. Lori and her death by fire meant nothing to that man. Conrad was not going to pay him more—not until he proved himself.

"Speak of the devil. Yeah, Simpson, what do you want?" His burner phone had rang right on cue.

"That Lori chick is on TV." Simpson was way too excited about that.

"She's supposed to be dead, you moron! What part of 'burned up in an accidental fire in a death trap apartment house' did you not understand?" he screamed at the man.

"I understood it all right, boss. I lit the match and threw the bottle into the apartment then took off back down the tree just like you told me to," he told the man as he rubbed at his skinned-up forearm. "I didn't know she ran out the door." Simpson was flustered and trying hard not to stutter. "She was in there. I saw her go in. And I waited till it got real quiet just like you told me."

Conrad Meyer could not believe how hard it was to find reliable help these days. "Lay low and stay out of sight till I contact you again," he finally said. Then he added, "Don't use this phone for anything. Don't call me or anyone else. I will call you!" And with that he hung up.

Matthew Simpson nervously scratched at the scrape on his forearm. It burned. He had washed it good with soap and water, but he didn't have anything to put on it—not even a lousy Band-Aid. And the boss didn't want him to go anywhere.

December turned into January and nothing new happened. Lori never walked anywhere alone anymore. Her boss had refused to let her pay rent, and the Boys had found her a small, clean efficiency apartment in a building near theirs. The second week of January, they had helped her move her meager possessions into it.

The following Sunday morning, Michah left for his two weeks in Florida. Marcus drove him to the airport before he went to pick up Lori and take her to church with him. He planned—and he hoped Lori was still in agreement—to take her furniture shopping after church. He was sure she was sleeping on the floor of her new efficiency apartment.

On the way to the airport, Michah had confirmed that he was going to buy a burner phone and contact Lori's brother, Todd, while he was in Florida. Marcus wasn't particularly comfortable with the plan, but he could not come up with an irrefutable reason not to do it. Neither he, or Michah had ever been made aware that Detective Mitchell and Lori's brother, Detective Wright, had joined forces and were working together on the Arnold case. Lori was not aware of it either.

"Stop worrying, big brother," Michah told him for the umpteenth time. "I'm not going to give anything away."

Marcus gave his twin a sidelong glance before exiting the highway and heading into the airport. "I know you don't plan to, Michah, but you seem to be discounting who you'll be talking to and who you're talking about. A lawman, trained to extract details. And a crook, who seems to have found her in spite of the lawman's efforts to hide her." He shrugged. "Just sayin'."

Michah ran a hand down his face. "You know this needs to be done. Lori's family needs to know she's safe—sort of." After a beat, he added, "I'd like to tell her brother, the detective, where to look for Maquire, but that would give too much away."

"We don't even really know if Maquire had anything to do with this," Marcus reminded him, referring to the bottle rocket that had been discovered as the source of the fire.

The car was quiet for a moment. Then Marcus spoke. "I know you're right," he admitted. "But things are quiet now. Maybe he scared her and then went away. Maybe he's done." Shrugging, he added, "It's not like nobody knows already that he's a bank robber and maybe a killer."

"Things that maybe they wouldn't know if she had just picked him up at the bank and taken him to the airport," Michah reminded him. "She's unfinished business."

The young men said their good-byes and Michah headed for his gate as Marcus headed back to the interstate. He was excited about the plans he and Lori had for the day. First, church. Then lunch at

The Diner. After that they were going to do a little shopping for Lori's new apartment.

As he thought about her new home—closer to him, cleaner, and hopefully safer—he couldn't help but smile. Even though he was sorry about the fire and all the fear it had caused Lori, he wasn't sorry she had a better place to live. He knew it was more expensive than her other rooms. And he knew she never would have moved there if she hadn't lost her other home.

He found it worrisome that all had been quiet in the few weeks since the fire. They still had no proof of who had started the fire. And even though the local police suspected Curtis Maquire of being the culprit, no one really knew. The DNA only proved that whoever started the fire had no previous record and no military or government jobs in his background. There were no fingerprints. Whoever was behind it was careful not to leave any.

No one even knew where Curtis Maquire was. Not for the first time, Marcus thought to himself that perhaps this was random. Perhaps the person who had lived there previously had enemies as well, and those enemies hadn't known Lori was the new tenant. A man could hope, couldn't he?

CHAPTER NINE

———†———

M ichah picked up his rental car and headed out of the airport. He found his hotel and, after unpacking, walked out and down to the beach. January in northern Florida wasn't particularly warm, and he was glad he had a coat. Still, it was nicer than Tulsa, and the ocean spread before him was beautiful.

After a long walk, he found his way to a small cafe and ordered his lunch. While he waited for the meal, he called his brother. "Hey! Big brother! It isn't true; Florida is not hot. At least not where I'm at. It's in the fifties. Maybe." He left a message.

Marcus called him back a little while later. Michah was making his way back to his hotel. "So you made it safe and sound." He heard the smile in his brother's voice. "Good to know."

"Yeah, and I'm really glad you talked me into bringing jeans and sweaters," Michah told him. "Hopefully it will warm up later in the week."

The brothers chatted for a few minutes. Michah reached his hotel and Marcus and Lori reached the discount furniture store. "I need to get her in there before she changes her mind about buying a new mattress." Marcus spoke softly to his brother. "Sleeping on the floor just isn't right. And I will not let her pick up a used one." He shuddered.

"Gross," Michah agreed. "Go. And tell her hi for me."

The two weeks in Florida went quickly for Michah. He was pleasantly surprised and very happy to be offered a position in the South American missions field, contingent on his graduation. It would be hard to put so much distance between himself and

Marcus. The two had been inseparable their entire lives. They both knew the day was coming, though.

The day before Michah flew out, he bought the burner phone and called the Pittsburgh Police Department. It took a few minutes to get through to Lori's brother, but finally he had him on the line.

"This is Detective Wright. How can I help you?" Lori's brother spoke quickly into the phone. He really didn't need another interruption this morning.

"Hi," Michah responded. "You don't know me, but I have some news I think you'll want to hear."

Todd rolled his eyes. This could take a while. "Okay, let's hear it." He tried to sound friendly, but he heard the sharpness in his tone.

"I am a friend of your sister Lori," Michah began.

Todd sat up straighter and pushed aside the papers in front of him, drawing his notepad toward him as he responded, "Is she okay?" So not what he meant to say.

Michah rushed to assure the man. "She's fine. I promise. I know it's safer not to share any information about where she is in case the line is tapped, but I just wanted you to know she is doing fine. She has a job, a decent place to live, and friends who really care."

Inhaling and then exhaling deeply, Todd responded, "That's good to know. And I appreciate your carefulness and your concern."

"Do you have any messages you would like me to give her?" Michah asked. He was enjoying this little bit of pretending he was FBI or CIA or something big and important like that. And he was being very careful not to give anything away. Marcus would be proud of him.

"Why are you really calling?" Detective Wright went all serious cop on him. "Who are you? What do you really want?" Todd had lost his composure. He was afraid the guy would hang up before the trace went through.

"What?" Michah was momentarily confused. Then the lightbulb came on. He was such an idiot! "No, no. You misunderstood. I'm sorry. I really am a friend and I really am just trying to let you know Lori is okay—without giving anything away." He shook his head and rolled his eyes at his own foolishness. Marcus would definitely not be proud of him!

"Oh. Okay . . ." Todd was hesitant, but maybe the guy was for real. He sure wasn't worried about being traced.

"Look. I'm sorry. I know this is a weird phone call." Michah tried to regroup and recover. "She doesn't even know I'm doing this, but I . . . we . . . care about her. And we know how much she misses her family. I am just taking advantage of what I saw as an opportunity to let you know she's okay." There. That was better. Maybe.

"Fine. Thank you." Todd was shaking his head. "Is there anything else?"

"No. Do you have any messages for her? I will tell her I called and give her the messages in a couple of days." Michah waited. When he realized he was holding his breath, he exhaled.

"Tell her we love her and we miss her too," Todd finally said.

"Okay then. Good-bye." Michah disconnected. After staring at the phone in his hands for a few moments, he dropped it to the concrete under his feet and then stomped on it. Hard. Several times. Then he picked up all the larger pieces and threw them into a nearby dumpster.

Todd sat lost in thought, wondering about that phone call for several moments. Then he picked up the phone and put a call through to Detective Stewart Mitchell of the Tulsa Police Department.

"Good morning, Detective Mitchell. Detective Wright from Pittsburgh here," Todd announced.

"Well, I'm not sure yet how good it is, but good morning to you too," Mitchell responded. The two had developed a friendly working relationship over the past couple weeks as they worked together to sort through the mess that was Charles Arnold aka Curtis Maquire.

"I just had the strangest phone call," Todd continued without preamble.

Mitchell listened carefully and had started to take notes when it suddenly dawned on him what was really going on, and he chuckled. "Where did the phone call come from?" he wanted to know.

"I've got my team working on it," Todd responded. "You got any ideas?" It sort of felt like the man did.

"If you find out the call came from the Jacksonville, Florida area, it's Michah Stout." Mitchell chuckled as he answered the other detective. "He's down there for a job interview, and it sounds like something he would do."

"Who is Michah Stout?" Todd wanted to know. "More importantly, are you sure my sister is okay?"

"Your sister is fine," the Tulsa detective rushed to assure his Pittsburgh counterpart. "And Michah Stout and his twin brother, Marcus, are both attending the seminary here. Both men are straight arrows and harmless—if not a little misguided, and unaware that you already know where your sister is." Still chuckling, Mitchell continued, "I think one of them, Marcus most likely, has the hots for your sister."

"What? No. No, no, no! She's very vulnerable right now and, most likely, still in danger." Todd was more upset than he cared to admit. He was already in danger of being pulled from the case because Lori was his sister. "If you think there's something going on, you have to stop it. Please." He scrubbed a hand down his face in frustration.

"Detective, I assure you, there is very little going on and nothing to stop. The Stout boys are honorable men. They walk out their faith. I know them both well. Michah works here as a 911 operator. Marcus cleans a bank. They are good men whom I trust." Detective Stewart Mitchell knew both men quite well, actually. He went to the same church they attended. And he spent all day, every day, doing his best to walk out his faith too.

Todd calmed and felt his tightened muscles relaxing. "Okay. If you're sure." He shook his head. *Who knew today was going to go this way?* "I'll get back to you if that trace comes from somewhere else."

"Yes, please do," Mitchell stated. "We will keep you posted on anything new that develops." Then he added, "When Michah gets back to town, I will have a word with him." The two men hung up.

Strange things were happening. Lori was sure of it. She just wasn't sure which of those strange things were really happening and which were products of her overactive and exhausted imagination.

She was used to seeing the police come in to The Diner occasionally for a meal or a cup of coffee. But there seemed to be at least one, if not two, there all the time now. Or at least the whole time she was there.

And every time she left or came back to her apartment, she would see one parked nearby. Detective Mitchell had promised her they would keep an eye out for her safety. It seemed they really were.

Marcus was by her side so often now that she was feeling like they were the twins. Almost. She felt how much he missed Michah during the two weeks he was gone. She missed him too. And she felt guilty about how much she enjoyed having Marcus all to herself.

The investigation into the fire at her apartment was going slowly. Too slowly. There didn't seem to be any leads at all. She knew they suspected Curtis—Charles Arnold—but only because she had mentioned him as a possible enemy. There was nothing solid. No evidence pointed to anyone. The intruder had scraped off some skin and left a minute amount of blood on a tree limb outside her window. But there were no matches in the system. Without a suspect, they could get no match.

Detective Mitchell had told Lori she needed to stay put while the investigation was open. He told her she could be arrested for contempt if she fled. Not wanting to add that fear to her list of them, she had begrudgingly stuck around. She was glad not to leave the friends, the new family, she had found. She was glad for an excuse to be with Marcus. And she didn't have any money to run with, anyhow.

In early February a second Tulsa bank was robbed. The lone watchman was knocked out and tied up. The safe was emptied of all the ten- and twenty-dollar bills.

Mitchell ran a hand through his hair, further mussing it up. He was tired. He had "bags under the bags under his eyes," as his Grandmother would say. The robbery ring was definitely responsible. There was a new twist this time, though. It was the first time they had stuck with only tens and twenties. Those would be the easiest to spend.

The second bank robbery had frightened Lori more than she had ever been frightened before in her life, and at this point in time, she had been frightened a lot.

Marcus and Michah stuck to her like glue. Her boss and all of her coworkers were on high alert. And Lori always saw an officer near her everywhere she went. She didn't go very many places, but a car would pass her or a uniform would walk down the opposite side of the street. Sometimes one would walk with her and chat with her. As much as she appreciated their concern, the whole thing unnerved her. And she learned how to thank God for it. She found herself talking to God more now than she ever had. She found it felt right to do so. And sometimes she would look at her circumstances and thank God for the peace and comfort she felt in spite of them. She was thankful finally to have Him present in her life in a real and tangible way. The church she went to now with the Boys was teaching her so much about love and grace that sometimes tears would well up in her eyes when she thought of how happy she was now — in spite of the terror she faced every day.

Detective Mitchell headed up the team that was tasked with solving the robberies. They gathered for a bull session every morning before they hit the streets. Since no new evidence and no prints or DNA matches were showing up, things were at a virtual standstill.

A few mornings after the second robbery, a rookie suggested having the banks that hadn't been hit put some kind of marking or dye on some of their tens and twenties and just keep them in the safe in an easy-access spot. If they were stolen, they could be found and maybe they would get a trail to follow. Mitchell spent most of the rest of that day putting that plan into action.

There were very few banks in the area that still had the older style of safes that could be opened with a stethoscope and a good ear. They were all on high alert. Fortunately, all the robberies were happening after hours. Mitchell was grateful for that; there was less danger of innocent people dying.

Conrad Meyer was angry, very angry. He knew he was being watched, or at least watched out for. Since Matt and Steve weren't smart enough not to peel off a hundred dollar bill when a ten would suffice, he told them to only take tens and twenties. Then his "girlfriend" called him three times in five minutes. He barely managed to get the safe open. He stepped away to deal with her problem and make her understand she couldn't call him like that. (What did she even want, anyway?)

Handing his backpack to Steve to fill up while he took care of her problems became a big problem for him. Steve stuffed his pack full of tens and twenties too. Curtis had intended to take all the hundreds he could stuff into it.

Now he was shorter on cash than he wanted to be. Next time, he would make up for it. But first he needed to dump the girl. Naive was necessary; needy was not.

CHAPTER TEN

———†———

I t was a particularly slow night at The Diner. A late spring thunderstorm rolled through and caused the temperature to plummet, sending the late-night shoppers, moviegoers, and hungry bar hoppers home to turn their furnaces back on and crawl into their beds. Lori had rolled enough silverware to last a week.

When the door opened, she glanced up and was not surprised to see Michah walk through it. "Hey! If you can find a table, have a seat. I'll be with you as soon as I get all these orders in to the cook," she teased as she looked around at the empty room.

"Oh, my!" He grinned. "I guess I'll keep it easy and just get the usual." Lori and the Boys were comfortable joking around with each other. Their friendship had solidified. They had grown close and tight.

"Coffee and two eggs over easy coming right up!" She stuck her head into the kitchen to tell the cook and then grabbed a mug and filled it from the fresh pot she had just made, knowing the Boys would soon show up.

"How are finals going?" she asked.

"They are almost gone. Thank the good Lord for that. I think I'm gonna graduate!" Michah downplayed how well he knew he was doing. "Marcus is gonna make it too." He smiled as Lori set his plate down. "Sit, Lori. You've got time to chat tonight." He patted the chair beside him.

Lori sat. She joined them anytime she wasn't busy now. "Where is Marcus?" she asked. He usually showed up a few minutes after Michah.

"I have no idea," Michah admitted. "Since it's cold and rainy, he may be sitting tight and staying warm and dry." Shaking his head, he added, "No sense of adventure."

The radio one of the two officers at the corner booth was wearing made a static noise as someone spoke to him. Lori jerked. Michah patted her shaking hand. Standing up, she tucked a wayward lock of hair behind her ear and hurried to the kitchen without a word, without a backward glance.

Michah heaved a silent sigh as his ears tuned to the voice coming from the radio. "Robbery in progress. Possible hostage situation. Unknown number of suspects. Possibly armed and dangerous."

"I need to go back to work." Michah threw some money on the table and headed for the door.

Officer Trey Smith, Michah's friend, stopped him. "You should stay here Michah. And keep everyone away from the windows," he directed as he charged out the door. It was only then that Michah saw the police cars blocking the street and officers with shields standing near the entrance to the bank across the street: the bank his brother worked at.

He felt, rather than saw, Lori come up beside him. An agonizing sob ripped from her throat as she pushed out the door and onto the street before Michah could grab her and hold her back, before he could even scream himself. Forgetting what Trey had told him, he raced out the door and followed Lori into the street.

The second Lori saw the flashing lights on the street in front of The Diner, she knew. They were robbing the bank. And Marcus was in there. Without thinking, she ran out the door. She heard a scream and then realized it was her.

"Stop!" an officer with a shield ordered and jumped in front of Lori, stopping her and causing Michah to run into her back and stop as well. "You both need to return to The Diner and stay away from the windows," he ordered.

Lori glared at him, temporarily speechless. Michah found his voice. "My brother is in there. He may be the hostage!"

"Return to the building. When we need you, we will find you."

Another officer, Trey's partner, quietly and quickly steered them out of harm's way. "We can't confirm there is a hostage," he said carefully to Michah.

"He always comes to The Diner during his break, and he didn't show up!" Lori was on the verge of hysterics.

"Lori, let's go inside so these folks can do their job without worrying about us." Michah realized the gravity of the situation, and putting a supporting arm around Lori's waist, he led her back into The Diner.

"But . . . what about Marcus? We need to get him out of there!" She was ashen and her words weren't making any sense. Michah pushed her through to the kitchen, where the crew and three other customers had chosen to hide out and try to stay safe.

"The police will get him out. He may not even be anywhere near the robbers. Maybe he's found a safe place to hide." Michah held her by the shoulders and looked into her eyes. Seeing the fear there, he continued to soothe. "It's a huge building. He could be all the way up on the eighth floor. And the safe is on the main floor." He thought this, but he really didn't know for sure.

"Break time!" Marcus pumped a fist and headed for the elevators. He could hardly contain himself.

A pastoral position had opened up in northern Illinois, near Chicago, and he had been offered the position. Neither Michah nor Lori knew yet. He planned to tell them now. He pushed the button for the lobby and watched the numbers descending: eight, seven, six, five, four, three, two, and lobby. The doors opened and he walked out and headed for the entrance. He could see The Diner. He could see the rain pouring down. He could not see Tim, the security guard, waiting there to let him out.

Something in his peripheral vision caused him to pause and glance toward the hallway that led to the vault. A scuffling noise turned him. Without even thinking about it, he walked into the hallway and called out, "Tim? Where you at? It's break time for me." His words were met with silence.

Another small shuffling sound from the vault room sent his pulse racing. Quietly he continued down the hall. There was no sign of Tim. Then he saw a light moving under the door to the vault room. *Why is Tim in there?* he wondered to himself.

He pushed the door open. "Hey, Tim. Can you let me out for break? I'll bring you back some pie."

Tim was seated on the floor with his mouth, wrists, and feet duct taped. Something hard pushed into Marcus's ribs, and a voice ordered him, "Go sit by your friend and don't try anything."

He was pushed to the floor and soon found himself being bound up the same way.

Looking heavenward, he prayed silently, *Father, protect us from harm.* Glancing at Tim, he now could see the man was hurt. The room's dim light showed a trickle of blood running down from a gash in the side of his head just above his ear. The man seemed dazed and was clearly terrified.

Marcus tried to communicate with his eyes. Looking at Tim, then at his wound, then back at Tim. How do you ask a question with only your eyes? Tim rolled his eyes and nodded in the direction of the man who had tied Marcus up. It was a pretty clear answer, so Marcus figured Tim understood the question.

"Get in here," a voice barked from the other side of a big steel door. Marcus knew that the actual vault was on the other side of the steel door. The man with the gun glanced at him and Tim and then disappeared through the door. He could hear their mumbled conversation but wasn't sure what was being said.

"We're taking fives and fifties this time," Conrad told Steve and nodded to the pile of banded bills left lying casually on a small table just inside the vault room. "I guarantee those are marked somehow. Probably all the tens and twenties."

Steve nodded. "'Cause that's all we took last time. Not as smart as we are, huh, boss?" the man nearly crowed.

"No, they're not." Conrad rolled his eyes. He really had to find smarter help.

Marcus worked at the tape on his face. His hands were behind his back, so all he could do was move his mouth around and rub his cheek on his shoulder. Tim was doing the same thing. Both men stopped when the gunman walked back through the door. Apparently satisfied, he left again.

Marcus got his loose enough to move his mouth and put it close to Tim's ear to whisper, "Are there only two?"

Tim nodded and worked his mouth and rubbed his shoulder with his cheek. "Both armed?" Marcus asked. Tim nodded again.

Marcus could see the man was in pain and struggling to stay alert. He wiggled around so he was closer to Tim and had his back up against his taped hands. "See if you can get the tape on my hands loose," he suggested.

Tim began to feel around Marcus's wrists, and finding a loose corner of duct tape, he tugged at it, beads of sweat rolling down the sides of his face. Marcus felt the tape coming loose. He reached his free hand into his back pocket and grabbed his phone. Not realizing how sweaty his hands had become, he pulled the phone out and it slipped from his grasp.

The small clatter it made must have been loud enough that the men in the safe heard it. Their muffled conversation ended. Marcus and Tim stilled and looked toward the door. Both the robbers exited carrying backpacks over their shoulders; they were bulging and obviously heavy.

They grabbed Marcus under the arms and dragged him into the vault, shutting the door behind them. He was locked in a pitch-black room. He had no idea what was going to happen to Tim. He started working fervently at the tape around his ankles. If he could just get his feet free, he could get out. He had to try to help Tim.

Marcus stood up and ripped the tape off his mouth. He felt his way to the wall and around it to the door. Trying to open it, he soon realized it was locked from the outside. He had no phone and no way out.

One of the men removed a large knife from his pocket and cut the tape off Tim's ankles, then the two of them stood him up. "Now it's time for you to get us out of here," the man who had opened the safe growled at him as he pushed him toward the hallway door.

Tim was dizzy. He was sure he had a concussion. He was barely able to keep his feet. He started walking toward the main entrance.

"Not so fast." He felt the gun poke him in the kidney. "We need the back door. The one the president comes in after he parks his

BMW" growly told him. Tim shook his head. He winced from the pain it caused. He didn't have a key to that door.

Growly ripped the tape off his mouth. "You better mind your manners. Don't make me regret letting you talk." Again the gun nudged him.

"I don't have a key for that door." He closed his eyes and took a deep breath. He was so dizzy.

"You better find one. Fast!"

Sweat poured off Marcus. He could not see at all. Time was slipping by. He was so hot he felt like closing his eyes and just going to sleep. He felt breathless. He knew he hadn't been locked in the safe long enough to use up all the oxygen, so he forced himself to stay alert. Knowing there was nothing else he could do, he sat down beside the door. He felt a little lightheaded, and after a while, pins and needles began shooting through his feet and lower legs.

Michah pulled his phone out and looked at it. No calls. No texts. And it was almost fully charged. He put it back in his pocket, a look of utter dejection on his face.

Lori saw Michah check his phone, and she saw the brief look of disappointment and fear on his face before he pocketed it again. She went to her locker and retrieved her phone. Nothing. She looked at Michah with the same hopelessness in her eyes he was feeling.

When had Marcus become so important to her? She reluctantly admitted to herself that she had fallen in love with him. She prayed she would see him again. She prayed he was safe.

Michah thought to call the station and explain to them why he had never come back from his break. He figured they already knew, and the phone call confirmed it.

He shut the phone and, leaning in, whispered in Lori's ear, "He's okay." In spite of his fears, his heart said his twin was okay. Sensing it was a twin thing, Lori didn't question Michah. She nodded and let out a breath. She never took her eyes off her phone.

"I have a key to the president's office. He may have a spare key there, but if he keeps his drawers locked, I won't be able to get it," Tim told the armed men.

A poke in the ribs reminded him they were armed. "Let's go to his office, then," growly man said. "Lead the way." Another poke and Tim was walking back to the elevators.

"His office is on the fourth floor," he told them, and growly voice pushed the button and the elevator ascended to the fourth floor.

Once the door to the bank president's office was unlocked, Tim was pushed to the floor and his mouth was taped shut again. "Stay put," the second man told him. They were both still wearing ski masks, and all he could see was their eyes. He hadn't seen them well enough to even know what color they were.

Tim was shorter than most men, only five foot seven. He was also, as his wife would say, a little "fluffy." She was a good cook. He hoped he lived to eat that leftover lasagna he'd been thinking about all night. Both men were several inches taller than him. Both men looked like they worked out. A lot.

He had seen no jewelry of any kind. No tattoos. Nothing to help identify them. He took a deep breath and tried to steady his breathing. His head hurt. He knew he had to stay awake and alert. How long did Marcus have before he ran out of oxygen? He really didn't know. He imagined, hoped, it would take a long time since he was locked in the vault alone.

"Hey, Con! Looky what I found!" the second man told growly voice. And Tim had a name.

Growly barked at the first man, "Watch it! You don't want me to have to kill the guard, do you?"

Tim was glad he was sitting—head down, eyes closed. He pretended he had passed out. "He's out, boss," second man said and kicked Tim's leg. "Get up. It's time to get us out of here."

"You idiot. His hands are still taped. Help him up!" growly barked and grabbed Tim's arm on one side while the other man jerked him up from the other side. They made their way back to the president's private entrance.

Growly pointed his gun at Tim's face and barked a question: "Now, which key unlocks this door?"

Tim stared at the keys. There were at least a dozen keys on the ring and six that could fit this door. They would have to try all six of them and hope one worked. One by one the keys were held up, and one by one he eliminated them. Most he just shook his head. Four times he nodded. The fourth time, the key fit.

Growly pushed Tim in front of him and shoved the door open. Tim shivered at the cold blast of air that hit him as he stepped out into the underground parking garage. It was eerily quiet. He could hear the rain coming down, running through the gutters, dripping somewhere. The press of a gun in his kidneys got him moving again.

A lone van was parked about ten feet from the door they came out of. It was black. Tim couldn't see any markings on it. He couldn't see the license plate from this angle either. The side door slid open and he was shoved inside. Growly voice followed, then the other man. The door hadn't even closed when the van took off, speeding toward the nearest exit.

A lone, unmarked, car rolled in front of the exit. Tim was on the floor in the back and could see nothing. He felt the van swing a hard left, going up on two wheels and nearly rolling. It threw him across the back and into the side of the van. Bruises were the least of his worries right now. He hoped he did hurt all over tomorrow. It would mean he was still alive.

Tim knew there were only two ways out of the garage. He was fairly certain the hard left had been because the first exit was blocked. Surely the second would be too? He didn't pray often. Not like his wife. But he was praying now. He really wanted to go home and hold her again, tell her he loved her. Finish off that lasagna.

It was then he remembered the fight they had this afternoon. He remembered he hadn't kissed her good-bye. And how long had it been since he told her he loved her? He figured she just knew. But after that fight? Well, maybe she didn't.

"Please get me out of this, God. I want to go home and love my wife better. I want to love You better too." He finally prayed, and peace washed over him. Tears flowed freely down his cheeks. He knew. He finally understood. God was with him. Tim had walked far away, but God had never gone anywhere.

The van screeched to a halt. Tim was thrown across the floor again, slamming into the back of the seat. "What now, boss?" a new voice asked.

The boss crawled around the seat and sat on the floor beside Tim. He ripped the tape off his mouth and shoved a phone in his face. "I'm calling 911. You are telling them you are a hostage and we have big guns and we will kill you if they don't let us out of here." And with that, he pushed the three numbers.

"Nine one one. What is your emergency?" a voice asked.

"H-hello. My name is Tim Carson. I'm the security guard at First Bank and Trust. I am a hostage in the van that is in the underground parking garage. If the police don't let us out, these men will kill me. They have big guns." He wanted to say more. He wanted to tell his wife he loved her. He wanted to tell the police to just shoot until they were all dead. He felt ready to meet his maker now.

He barely got those few sentences out before the phone was snatched away from his face and turned off. "Go," growly voice said. "Drive toward the exit." He returned to his seat and readied his weapon.

The van crept forward and Tim prayed.

CHAPTER ELEVEN

———— † ————

B renda awoke with a start. What was it? She lay there silently listening for a moment. All was quiet. She could still hear the rain coming down. And the drip. The constant drip from the gutters that Tim never cleaned. Never.

She remembered their fight about those gutters this afternoon. He had left for work without kissing her good-bye. He never did that unless he was really mad. And she knew she had made him really mad.

He had never cleaned the gutters out last fall. Not even once. Now here it was spring, and they were full of leaves from last fall. Water poured over the sides everywhere. Sighing, she got out of bed. Holding on to anger would not help her sleep. A glance at the clock told her it was after two. Maybe she should call him.

What would she say, though? She knew last fall had been crazy. She knew that every single weekend something had happened. His mom had been sick. They had kept the grandkids. It had rained. There was a wedding. She knew he had never had a chance to clean those gutters. And so far there hadn't been a chance to do it this year.

So why was she angry with him? Why was she riding him so hard about it? *I need to apologize*, she decided, and called his number. It rang until it went to voice mail. She left a message. "Tim, I'm sorry. You were right; you really never did get a chance to do the gutters. I shouldn't have jumped on you about it. I love you. Please, call me back." She dropped to the sofa and set the phone down beside her. After picking up the remote and turning on the television, she covered up with the old afghan that was always on the couch, the one Tim always slept under when he napped in the afternoon.

Flipping through the channels, she finally stopped on one that played local news. The rain was in the forecast for the foreseeable future. Nothing new there. She was about to change the channel again when a news blip began rolling across the bottom of the screen.

It said, *A bank robbery is in progress at the downtown branch of the First Bank and Trust. Police have surrounded the building and there are apparently hostages.*

Brenda sat up and turned up the volume. At that moment the blip became live news. A male newscaster stood in the rain with the bank and flashing lights from several first-responder vehicles in the background. He went on for several minutes about the lack of information he had. Apparently even law enforcement had very little information. They knew there were two civilians inside and three known perpetrators.

"Word has been received that one person has been taken hostage by the robbers," the newsman said. "The man called 911 a couple minutes ago," he added.

Brenda realized it had to be Tim. He may have been mad enough not to kiss her good-bye, but he would never be mad enough not to call her if he could to tell her he was okay. She called her pastor.

"Hello?" he answered on the second ring.

"Pastor, it's Brenda Carson," she said.

"Tim is the hostage." He knew. "I'm already praying. And Michelle is on the phone getting the prayer chain going," he added.

"Thank you," she told him. Tears tracked down her face and plopped silently on the afghan. "Pastor, we fought before he left. It was so stupid. But I was so angry . . ."

"Brenda, it's going to be okay. God's got this. God's got him. And He's got you too."

Brenda was already off the sofa and headed for the bedroom before she realized she had moved. "I'm going down there," she said.

"I'll meet you there," her pastor told her, and they both hung up.

Brenda pulled on the jeans and sweatshirt she had discarded the night before. She stuffed her feet into boots and grabbed a jacket.

Her keys and purse were by the back door, and she snagged them on her way out. The garage door was barely up before she floored it down the driveway and onto the street.

The streets were quiet this time of night. Everyone was home in their beds, as they should be. The closer Pastor Victor got to downtown, the more traffic he saw. He imagined at least a few of those cars were unmarked police cars. He was stopped two blocks from the bank and ordered to leave.

"Officer, I'm Pastor Steven Victor. Tim Carson, the hostage, is one of my flock. His wife, Brenda, is down here someplace and I'm supposed to meet her," he told the man in blue. Then he showed him his license and pastoral credentials.

The officer spoke into his shoulder mic. Then he instructed the Pastor: "Someone will be here in a moment to walk you in. Please wait in your car."

"Yes, sir," he said, and settled back in his seat to pray again. "Father, protect these servants of Yours. Keep them from harm. Give them wisdom to know what to do."

"Pastor Victor?" a voice asked. A very tall man stood outside his car looking down into the driver's-side window.

"Yes. Detective Mitchell? I'm here for Brenda. Tim's in there," Pastor Victor explained.

Detective Mitchell went to the church he pastored, so it was a relief to see a familiar face working the scene. "Come with me," the detective said, and then turned and started down the street. Victor hurried to follow him.

Save for the chatter of the radio mic attached to the detective's shoulder, they walked in silence down an alley. Halfway down the block, they crossed a street and continued walking down the alley. The man stopped at a door and rang a bell. When a face looked out the small window, he flashed his badge. The door opened.

The detective walked away with a brief wave as he spoke into his microphone. Pastor Victor entered a very clean and tidy storage room. A large woman wearing an apron ushered him through to a kitchen. It was then he realized he was in The Diner. The scent of fresh-baked pies tickled his nose.

"Pastor!" He looked toward the voice and saw Michah Stout, his friend Lori, and Brenda huddled in a corner together. After hugging Brenda and reassuring her again, he shook Michah's hand and gave Lori's shoulder a brief squeeze.

"What are you two doing here?" he asked.

"Marcus is in there," Michah told him quietly. Fresh tears slid down Lori's cheeks as she and Brenda continued to cling to each other.

The Pastor blanched as he realized this was also the bank Marcus worked as a janitor at. "Oh!" he stated, the surprise and shock evident in his voice. "We need to keep praying." And with that he went to his knees. Closing his eyes, he heard the rustle of several more bending knees as he began to pray again.

The van crept forward. Evidently the 911 operator had relayed his message. When the driver suddenly floored it, Tim was thrown back against the back doors of the van. "Get us out of here!" the growly voice ordered. The van raced through the night. Tim had no idea where they were going beyond the first left out of the parking garage.

He counted two more lefts and then a couple rights. Then he lost track. He couldn't have said what streets they were traveling, so why would it really matter? Somehow he knew it should, but his head hurt too bad to care. After what seemed like hours but was, in fact, only about half an hour, the van made one more right turn onto a road that was very bumpy. If Tim had to guess, he would say it wasn't even paved.

"Make sure he doesn't have his phone and dump him out here," the growly voice said. Tim knew they thought he had passed out. He thought he probably had as well and decided to pretend to still be out.

His pockets were searched and his phone removed. "Just take out the battery and throw it away. He can keep the phone."

The side door was thrown open and the battery sailed through the air. The van continued on down the road a short distance. *What a nice guy*, Tim thought to himself. Hope welled deep inside. He really thought he was going to live through this after all.

The van stopped and the side door slid open again. This time Tim was shoved out, hands still bound. He felt his phone being stuffed in between them. Before the door was even shut, the van was off, down the road again.

With his hands bound behind him, he struggled to stand up and then he started walking back in the direction from which they had come.

He was on a rural two-lane road. Deep potholes attested to a lot of heavy equipment use and very little maintenance. Fences lined each side of the road and the dark shapes behind them were silent, apparently sleeping, cattle.

An owl hooted from a distant tree. A dog—or coyote—ran across the road in front of him. Tim was not a country boy, and everything terrified him. A strong odor assaulted his nose. A skunk. He walked past it and realized the van had hit it. Maybe the smell would linger long enough they could use it as evidence? He thought so, but he wasn't sure. How long did that smell last?

The rain had finally, thankfully, stopped. At least it wasn't raining here. A full moon was on a downward march. It was his only light, but it was enough. He could see the road he was walking on. He really didn't want to see anything else.

Something glinted in the road ahead of him, just a flicker. He figured he was imagining things but kept his eyes focused on that spot anyhow. A few more steps and he knew it wasn't his imagination. It was a knife. Did it slip out of the van when they opened the door to throw out his cell phone battery?

Tim eased down in the middle of the road with his back to the knife. Somehow, he got a grip on it and got it turned so he could cut the tape that still held his hands bound. In spite of the chill in the air, Tim was sweating as he sawed. Sweat ran down his face and blurred what little vision he had. His hands were slick with sweat. After he nicked himself a couple times, he figured his hands had more than sweat on them. He thought, too late, that whatever fingerprints had been on the knife would be long gone now.

He sawed away and nicked himself a few more times but finally broke free of the heavy tape. Carefully he wrapped the tape up and stuffed it in his pocket. Fingerprints? Doubtful. They wore gloves in the bank. But he wasn't going to take a chance of losing any evidence.

He pocketed his phone, which he had somehow managed to keep tucked between his hands as he walked. Briefly he wondered if he could find the battery. He walked back and forth across the road several times for about thirty feet before and after the spot where he found the knife. If the battery was there, it wasn't going to be an easy find. The moon was almost gone when Tim started down the road again. Farmers got up early, he thought. Someone would find him soon.

Sergeant Mason spoke into his shoulder mic: "Subjects have left the bank in a black Ford panel van. No markings. License plate unreadable. Headed north on Main. Pursue with caution. Hostage on board." Responses crackled through the mic from several different undercover vehicles.

"Where's Mitchell?" the sergeant wanted to know. The mic crackled again. "Tell him we're going in."

Several remaining members of the force approached the bank entrances and quietly, carefully began to clear the building.

"First floor clear," Sergeant Mason's mic crackled. "We found a cell phone on the floor outside the vault."

"Has the bank president gotten here yet?" Mason spoke into his mic.

"He hasn't answered his phone yet, Sergeant," the voice crackled through the mic.

"Well, then send somebody to his house and tell them to get the man out of bed and drag him down here. We need him *now*!"

Finding the cell phone outside the vault led him to wonder if there was someone inside it. "Whose phone is it?" he asked.

"We're calling the last number dialed to find out," a voice spoke through the mic. "Hang on."

Mason counted to five and the officer came back on. "We just confirmed the phone belongs to Marcus Stout. He's the janitor."

Unbeknownst to Sergeant Mason, Detective Mitchell had walked up beside him. When he turned his head, sensing someone there, he saw the man, saw the look on his face. "Get that president here ASAP!" he ordered.

"Does anyone know if that vault is vented?" Mitchell wanted to know. Mason shook his head.

The detective strode off toward the main entrance. Mason saw him go in and head toward the hall that led to the vault. He hurriedly followed him inside.

Michah's cell phone rang. It was Marcus. He quickly put it on speaker and answered it as Lori crowded closer to hear. "Marcus! Brother, are you okay? What's going on? Where are you?" The questions spilled out rapid-fire.

"This is Officer Trey Smith. Is this Michah Stout?" the officer wanted to know.

"Yes, this is Michah. Where's Marcus? You're on his phone." Michah's confused look sent fresh tears down Lori's cheeks. "Please tell me what's going on." His voice shook when he spoke.

"We found a cell phone and we're just verifying who it belongs to," Trey told Michah. "That's all I can tell you for now," he said, and then when his mic crackled, he hung up abruptly.

"Boss, we have a situation," crackled across Sergeant Mason's shoulder mic.

"What?" Mason barked back.

"Mr. Drake is missing. His wife too," the voice spoke quietly. Only Mason could hear it. "It looks like their evening meal was interrupted. The back door was left open. Two half-finished meals on the table. A chair tipped over. A water glass broken on the floor. Both cell phones, a purse, and two sets of keys on the counter. Both cars in the garage. We will find someone to open that vault, sir."

Could this night possibly get any worse? the Sergeant wondered, not for the first time. And it only took a moment for him to realize that the MO had changed again. No one had been locked in the safe before. And no bank presidents had gone missing.

Brenda, Lori, Michah, and Pastor Victor huddled together in a corner booth of The Diner. Statements had been taken from everyone, and they were all allowed to leave. The staff had stayed to finish their shifts and feed the officers who were still there working the scene. The place still wasn't particularly busy, so Lori sat with her friends and alternated between ringing her hands in despair and praying for Marcus and Tim's safety.

It was dark and quiet and getting really stuffy in the vault. Marcus hoped he was imagining it, but he felt like it was getting harder to breath. He remained seated on the floor and calmed himself reciting the twenty-third Psalm over and over in his head. He feared speaking it out loud would use his oxygen up more quickly, but he really didn't know. It seemed like hours had passed when in reality it could have been only minutes. Eventually he lay down and closed his eyes. He was so tired.

"Sergeant Mason?" A rookie cop Mason didn't know approached him with an older gentleman beside him. "This is Matthew Ryan, retired bank president."

Ryan held out an arthritic hand, and Mason shook it gently. "I'm here to help in any way I can," the older gentleman stated simply, a tremor in his voice. "Tim started working here two years before I retired seven years ago. He's a good man."

"So is the man we think is locked in the safe," Mason responded.

"Oh, dear," Ryan muttered as the rookie walked away.

"Is he in danger of suffocating? How much time does he have?" Mason wanted to know.

"He is in danger, yes. It's an older safe. No vents. If he stays quiet, doesn't have any fear of closed spaces or the dark, he should be able to survive several hours," Mr. Ryan told him. Then he asked, "He doesn't have asthma or any other health issues, does he?"

Mason shook his head. "I don't know, but I know how to find out." And he pressed his mic to call a blue to go and question Michah Stout.

"And it only takes one person with the combination to open it." Eyeing Mason, the older man continued to answer the Sergeant's questions. "No, I don't know the combination. They would have changed it after I retired." Shaking his head, he added, "I tried to talk the board into upgrading the safe, and they refused. Said it was too expensive. Said it wasn't really necessary. They might change their minds now."

Silence fell between the sergeant and the retired bank president, both lost in their own thoughts for a moment. Mason finally broke the silence: "I need a list of all the people you think might know that combination."

"Got pen and paper?" Ryan asked, looking down at the house-coat and slippers Mason had not noticed before. "I'm not as well prepared for taking notes as I usually am."

Mason handed him the items and apologized for dragging him out so quickly in the middle of the night. "The Diner is open if you would like to sit in there where it's warmer." The sky chose that moment to burst open again. "And dryer," Mason added, and walked with the man across the street.

Finding Detective Mitchell inside talking to Michah Stout, Mason walked up to them and asked Michah about Marcus's health and any fears of claustrophobia or darkness. Feeling somewhat reassured by the brother's answers, believing that Marcus had a good chance of surviving, Mason treated himself to a cup of coffee and a few minutes out of the rain while he and Detective Mitchell talked to Mr. Ryan and went over the very short list he presented them with.

Lori sat quietly while Detective Mitchell and Sergeant Mason talked to Michah. The questions they were asking frightened Lori at first. When she realized that the answers meant Marcus should be okay, she began to relax. And realizing the detective was a Christian, recognizing him from church, she thanked God for the grace she was able to see now in this situation.

The sky was beginning to lighten. Tim wasn't sure what time it was or how far he had walked. His head hurt. He was so tired. One foot in front of the other took everything he had. He felt sick. Even thinking about the lasagna made him queasy. Surely he was getting closer to civilization?

A wrought-iron fence along the left side of the road caught his attention. Shafts of early sunlight glinted off the tombstones. The brightness hurt his head. He looked away. Something seemed off, so he looked back. It wasn't the sun bouncing off a tombstone; it looked like someone was trying to signal. He stared at the spot until he could make out shapes and movement. Two figures were sitting against a large stone. One held something bright in their hand and moved it back and forth occasionally, reflecting the light from the rising sun.

Tim wasn't sure what he was going to find, what he was getting himself into, but he figured he might as well have a look. If someone really wanted him dead, he thought he already would be.

The couple was tied up together and separately. Ropes held their ankles and wrists out in front of them. Another rope was wrapped around both of them and the tombstone. Their heads were loosely covered with paper sacks and their mouths were taped shut. A large diamond ring flashed in the sun, blinding Tim and sending shards of pain through his head.

Carefully he removed the sack and the tape from the woman and then the man. "What happened?" he asked.

"We were kidnapped and dumped in this cemetery last night," the woman said, fear in her voice and eyes.

"I have a knife in my pocket," Tim told them. "I'm going to get it out and cut your ropes."

"Please," the man spoke. "Do you have a cell phone?" The man looked at Tim and blinked. "Tim?"

"Yes. How . . .?" Recognition dawned in Tim's eyes. "Mr. Drake! Mrs. Drake!" Shaking his head and then groaning because it hurt, he began working on the man's ropes. "This cannot be a coincidence that they dumped me out so I would walk past this place."

"No, I don't believe so either," Mr. Drake responded, then asked again, "Do you have a cell phone?"

"I have a phone, but they tossed the battery out of the van. I tried to find it, but no luck." Tim worked quietly for a moment. "I did find the knife. I don't think they meant for it to slide out when they tossed the battery, though."

"They robbed the bank last night," Mr. Drake said. It wasn't a question.

"Yes, they did. And they locked Marcus in the safe." Tim helped Robert Drake stand up, groaning inwardly as the weight wrenched his shoulders and the pain shot up his neck and through his head. The two of them helped Angela Drake to her feet and she stood, clinging desperately to her husband's arm.

"He will suffocate if they can't get him out." Robert took a couple steps in the direction of the road. Angie clung to him and Tim followed close behind the pair.

Realizing Mr. Drake was planning on walking for help, Tim asked, "Should we take the ropes and sacks with us? Evidence?"

"No. Let's leave it to mark where we were sitting," Mr. Drake responded after a thoughtful moment.

"Okay." Tim shrugged and kept walking. "What were you signaling with?" he wanted to know.

Mrs. Drake turned and looked askance at him. "Signaling? We didn't even know anyone was around. We had nothing to signal with." Still looking at him, she pushed a lock of hair behind her ear and bright white fire shot from her left hand. Tim put up a hand to block the light and the pain it sent through his eyes.

"Your ring! That's what I saw! The sun hits your ring and it flashes so bright I could have seen it from the moon," Tim said excitedly.

Mrs. Drake looked at the four-carat diamond on her ring finger. "I just had it cleaned. Is it really that bright?" she asked.

"Yes" was all Tim could say in answer. He knew God was involved. The kidnappers could not have planned on him seeing her ring glinting in the sun. And he wondered that she still had the ring. Why hadn't the thieves taken it? It had to be worth thousands of dollars.

Mr. Drake stopped and held a hand up. "I think I hear someone coming." Tim heard it too.

"Do you think those men are back? Shouldn't we hide?" Mrs. Drake looked around nervously.

There was no place to hide. The threesome stood off to the edge of the narrow road and waited.

An ancient pickup truck that probably used to be red soon came into view. It slowed and then came to a noisy halt in front of them. "Can I help you folks?" An older man with gray hair sticking out from under an ancient ball cap bearing a seed company advertisement eyed them warily. He had a full beard and was wearing an old patched and stained pair of bib overalls. That, and the beat-up thermos and a lunch pail on the seat beside him, attested to the probability that he was a farmer heading out to his fields for the day.

"Please." Mr. Drake spoke first. "If you have a cell phone, will you call the local police and tell them you found us."

The old man dug an ancient and battered flip phone from the pocket of his bibs and tapped in a number. His nails were longer than was decent for a man and seemed permanently stained with dirt and grime. "Hey, I got some lost folks out here on the old Cemetery Road about two miles out from my house. Can you come pick them up?" He listened a moment and responded. "Could be. There's three of them. Two men and a woman."

Eyeing the bank president he asked, "You Drake?"

"Yes. Yes, I am."

"Okay. I'll tell them." The man flipped his phone shut and put his truck in gear. "Sheriff says he's on his way." And with that he headed on down the road, apparently unwilling to stay and get involved any more than he already had.

"Thank you!" Mrs. Drake called after the retreating truck. The old man stuck an arm out the window and gave a brief wave before he disappeared around a bend in the road.

"So I guess we just stand here and wait?" Tim wondered.

"No," Drake responded. "We walk back toward the cemetery and wait there." He started the short walk back. Mrs. Drake and Tim followed.

"You folks doin' all right?" the young deputy asked. He had taken only a few minutes to arrive, and his patrol car had barely stopped before he was out and walking around it toward the three-some sitting on tombstones near the road. None had the energy left to stand.

"We're alive," Mr. Drake responded.

"Tell me what happened—short version for now," the deputy requested.

They gave a brief statement, and the young lawman called in a team to process the scene. "Let's get y'all back to town," he finally said.

"Please." Drake spoke to the deputy as soon as they were en route. "I need to go to the bank immediately. I have to open the safe and let someone out before he suffocates."

A brief glance sideways at the bank president and the deputy reached over and flipped on the lights. Flooring it, he made the trip to the bank in record time.

During the trip, the three continued to share what they remembered about their abductors. Tim wondered if there was a reason why the Drakes were tied to that particular stone and stated vehemently that he believed they were left where he would find them.

Tim also turned over the tape he had saved and the knife. "I'm really sorry that I messed up any fingerprints that might have been on it," he told the deputy, explaining that he had used the knife to free his hands and the Drakes'.

The deputy was quick to reassure him that the likelihood of there having been any prints on the knife was slim to nothing. "They probably never took their gloves off," he added.

The last thing Tim remembered to tell the man was about the skunk they had hit. The young deputy responded with a chuckle and an affirmation that Tim was indeed correct—the smell did last a long time and could be helpful in identifying the van. "Very helpful," he assured Tim.

EMTs were standing by when the deputy's car screeched to a halt in front of the bank. Tim's head was screaming with pain from the wail of the sirens that had been turned on when they entered the city limits. He sat still, eyes closed, for several minutes after the car stopped and the sirens were silenced.

Drake jumped out before the car was even out of drive and hurried toward the bank's main entrance. Detective Mitchell met him at the door and the EMTs followed close behind. Sergeant Mason helped Mrs. Drake out of the car and ushered her into The Diner. He spoke briefly into his shoulder mic and a lone EMT ran to the cruiser to assist Tim.

Mr. Drake's hand shook as he worked through the combination. The first time through, he missed it. Closing his eyes and taking a few deep breaths and then letting them out slowly, he calmed himself and tried again. This time he heard the click of the lock disengaging. Two deputies pulled the heavy door open.

Marcus lay on the floor. He did not move when the lights came on. The EMTs jumped into action. He had a pulse, but it was weak. He was no longer sweating. His skin was dry and pale. They hooked him up to the portable oxygen and loaded him in the truck, heading to the hospital. Michah jumped in with him.

Tim was loaded into another rescue vehicle. Brenda climbed in with him, and they followed close behind the first. The Drakes were in good shape all things considered, but an EMT insisted on checking them out thoroughly at the scene.

Lori followed Pastor Victor to his car, and they headed to the hospital. It had been a full six hours since the robbery.

CHAPTER TWELVE

———————†———————

The black van seemed to have vanished into thin air. Somehow it had evaded all of the unmarked cars that were placed around the bank's perimeter in the hopes they could follow it out. Apparently the thieves knew where law enforcement would set up and had planned a route to successfully avoid them. An APB was issued and car washes and detailers were alerted to report any black vans that came in smelling of skunk.

"We're missing something," Detective Stewart Mitchell said thoughtfully. His eyes never left the papers and pictures spread out on the desk in front of him. Footage from bank security cameras provided very little information beyond knowing the thieves were pros.

"I think Carson had something when he said he believed they left him on that road so he would find the Drakes." Sergeant Mason bent over the photos as well. "Good thing the missus has such a flashy ring, huh?"

A thought crossed his mind. "Hey, Mitchell, how do you think the missus managed to keep that ring? It's obviously worth a small fortune." He also wondered out loud, "Do you think she's in on it? They got the combination somewhere?"

Detective Mitchell shook his head. "I kind of doubt she's in on it; she would have made sure they took the ring so she would look innocent." He shook his head. "These guys are smart enough to know better than to take something that hard to fence. Cash is virtually untraceable usually."

"Too bad they didn't take that pile of marked bills the banks were all told to set up," Mason complained.

Changing the subject, the detective glanced over his shoulder at the sergeant. "Ask the Drakes if they ever heard of Ralph or Judith Simpson. Maybe they could go through bank records too, see if there's a connection." Mitchell's gut was telling him there was something significant about the tombstone they had been tied to.

Mitchell's phone rang. "Yeah, Mitchell here," he said, a tone of distraction in his voice as he continued to stare at the photos. "Okay, thanks." He hung up.

"Hey, Mason, where'd you say the Stouts were from?" he asked and looked sharply at the sergeant.

After quickly flipping through his notes, Mason responded, "Norman."

"So were the Simpsons." Mitchell grew thoughtful again. "It's too crazy." He shook his head.

"Stout's awake. Doctor says we can talk to him." Mitchell stuffed his arms into his coat and pushed his hat down on his head. "You coming?"

Mason grabbed his coat and the files that were spread out in front of him and followed Mitchell out the door. "Heard anything on Carson yet?" he wanted to know.

"No, but I expect he'll be fine." Mitchell shook his head. Tim Carson had stood strong through six hours. And he had a head injury. "Paramedics said he passed out as soon as the patrol car stopped in front of the bank."

"I suppose it's too early to expect anything back from forensics on the tape or the knife," Mason mused aloud. Mitchell just shook his head and kept walking.

Mitchell thought to tell Mason, "They took fives and fifties this time."

Mason grunted his displeasure. "It would have been too good to be true . . ."

"Mr. Stout?" The detective's face swam in front of Marcus's eyes. He kept them open and tried to focus.

"Hey, bro. If you're not up for this yet, I'll make him leave." He heard Michah's voice and turned his focus so he could see his twin.

"What do you need to know?" Marcus asked, finding the detective again with eyes that were still blurred, his voice raspy and faint. He cleared his throat.

"Can you tell us what happened? Short version is good for now. We just need something to start with." Detective Stewart Mitchell could see Marcus wasn't up for much right now. And he knew he would get everything he could give them when he was up for it.

Marcus gave a brief statement. He ran through being bound up beside Tim and trying to communicate with tape over their mouths. He told what he knew of the two robbers. There were two of them and, according to Tim, both were armed.

"They locked me in the safe and took Tim as a hostage to help them get out of the building." He stopped talking and looked hard at Mitchell. "Is Tim okay?" he wanted to know.

"He's got a nasty bump on his head, but he's gonna be just fine," the detective told him. Marcus breathed a sigh of relief.

"One more question and I'll let you get some rest." Mitchell looked at his notes, but it wasn't because he needed to. He wanted Marcus and Michah to get a sense of the importance of the question he was about to ask. "Have you ever heard of Ralph or Judith Simpson?"

The twins looked at each other, and then, as Marcus continued to look at his brother, Michah answered the question. "Ralph was the preacher at a church we went to when we were kids," he told the detective. "Why? What do they have to do with the bank being robbed"

"We're not sure they have anything to do with it at this point." Mitchell weighed his options and his words carefully before he continued. "Could just be a crazy coincidence." He shrugged, handed Marcus his card, and headed for the door. "If you think of anything, call me. I will be in touch again soon, maybe later today." And with that, he slipped out the door.

Michah looked at Marcus and nodded before he opened the door and followed Mitchell down the hall. "Detective Mitchell! Hold up a minute." He tried to keep his voice low enough not to disturb anyone, but the man was flying down the hall and Michah really needed to talk to him. How could the Simpsons be involved in this? Why were they back on the twins' radar again after all these years?

The detective stopped and turned around, waiting for Michah to catch up before he punched the down button for the elevator.

"Why do you think the Simpsons are involved?" he wanted to know. The door had barely closed behind them.

Reaching in front of Michah, Mitchell pushed the stop button on the elevator and the descent halted. "We aren't releasing any-thing to the press yet, so I need your assurances that no one else—including your brother—will hear what I'm going to tell you." Mitchell stared hard at Michah. "Your brother isn't in any condi-tion to be trusted to remember not to say anything. Are you?" He needed to know.

Michah gulped, his Adam's apple bobbing. "Okay. I'll tell him you didn't tell me anything I can share." Shrugging, he added, "If he questions that, then I'll have to tell him that I just can't tell him anything."

Detective Mitchell shared with Michah that the Drakes had been tied to the Simpsons' tombstone. "It could be just a coinci-dence, but it seems unlikely. We don't really have any answers yet," he told Michah and then pushed the button and the elevator slipped on down toward the main floor.

Michah hit the stop button. Something needed to be said. "Ralph Simpson went to prison. He died there." Michah heaved a breath and continued. "It was because of what he did to Marcus and me and a dozen other children from that church."

The Detective waited quietly as Michah worked through the sordid tale. "Unusual to pop back up this many years later," he thought out loud. "Definitely not a coincidence." Pushing the down button, the elevator completed its descent.

"Thank you for sharing that," Mitchell told him. "You have my word I will be very discreet with that information," he added as the elevator doors slid open.

Mitchell exited and Michah pushed the button to go back to the fourth floor, grateful that the detective understood the angst that sharing that story could cause. He was truly puzzled. He agreed with Mitchell—this was no coincidence.

Sergeant Mason met the detective near the information desk in the hospital lobby. "Carson got his wound checked out. No internal bleeding. No permanent damage. They stitched him up and are keeping him in twilight for a few more hours so his brain will rest. Doctor says we can maybe talk to him this evening."

When Michah exited the elevator, he saw Lori standing hesitantly in front of the door to Marcus's room. She was wringing her hands and occasionally brushing her cheeks with them. He knew she was crying. Hurrying up to her, he took her hand and ushered her into his brother's room. Hospital staff had insisted "family only"; Lori was family. And seeing her was a lot less stressful than seeing the detective and answering his questions.

"Come on, Lori. Marcus will want to see you as badly as you want to see him," he told her as he pulled her into the room.

Brushing one last tear from her cheek, Lori took Marcus's hand and stood beside his bed, willing his eyes to open. They did.

"Hey." He spoke softly, his voice still raspy. "Are you okay?" he needed to know.

"I am now," she answered. "I'm glad to see you're okay too." She squeezed his hand and he squeezed back. His eyes fluttered shut again.

Moments later they popped open again. "I got a job in Chicago," he remembered. "I was going to tell you during my break, and then . . . everything else happened." His eyelids fluttered and closed again and he missed the look Michah and Lori shared.

"That's wonderful, Marcus." Lori's voice shook with a sob she refused to release.

"Glad to know it, big brother!" Michah spoke with excitement tempered by the look he saw on Lori's face. "Glad to know you'll be able to support yourself after I'm gone."

Marcus slept. And he dreamed he was asking Lori to marry him and go with him to Chicago. The dream was so real he would believe for a long time that it had really happened.

"Mr. Carson?" Detective Mitchell was back. The doctor had given him permission to speak briefly with Tim. He stood politely just outside the door to Tim's hospital room.

Two hours earlier Tim had woken up and remembered one of the robbers calling the other one "Con." He thought it was important and had told Brenda to call the detective immediately.

"Detective." Tim spoke softly; loud still hurt his head. "I remembered one of the robbers called the other one "Con." I think Con was the boss. Con had a real growly voice, raspy. Deep too. I'd know it if I heard it again."

Mitchell stayed a few minutes and made a few notes. When Tim thought to ask about fingerprints, he told him the truth: they were still waiting for that information to come back to them. "It could be a couple of days," he said. "And if there's no match in the system then, we are still on square one," he added.

"Thank you, Mr. Carson. Having a name is the biggest break we've had so far. And voice recognition could be a big help too." His phone rang and he glanced down at it before tipping his hat toward Brenda and striding out of the room and down the hall.

CHAPTER THIRTEEN

————†————

M atthew Simpson rubbed his hands together and chuckled softly. They had pulled it off. *He* had pulled it off. Those Stout boys were gonna get the message. And so what if that cute little Lori chick wasn't dead yet? She would be soon enough. And in the meantime, he had plans in the works to have some real fun with her. He chuckled again. He just had to be patient. That's what his daddy always told him: "Just be patient."

He still couldn't believe they had lost his knife. It had been his daddy's knife. It was all he had left of his daddy. Those Stout boys had taken him away. Now they were going to pay. He wished they hadn't lost his knife, and he really hoped the boss wouldn't find out they lost it. Con would really be mad.

The next morning, Marcus was released from the hospital and told to stay home and take it easy for the rest of the week. He did stay home from work and he did miss his classes, but Michah had brought his homework home to him and he was trying to stay caught up. Mostly the work just swam in front of his eyes.

Lori sat with him when she was off work. That wasn't very often, but it gave Michah a break from worrying about his twin. And when Lori was with him, Marcus wasn't worrying about her.

"Did I tell you the church is in Centerville? It's close to Chicago." Marcus kept talking about his new job. "They told me they have a three-bedroom parsonage. It's got two bathrooms and a two-car garage. And it's next door to the church, so one car will be enough because I can just walk to work, but there's room to store Michah's car for him. He said he wants us to drive it sometimes just so it doesn't quit running."

Lori smiled and reminded Marcus, "Yes, you told me. It all sounds really exciting." Whimsically, she added, "I've never been to Chicago before." She hoped Marcus would actually invite her to go with him.

"I've never been there either, so it's gonna be fun exploring it." He smiled that huge, dimpled smile before he added, "Of course it's gonna be a few months before there will be time for a vacation."

Finals were over and Marcus and Michah had both done very well. The graduation ceremony was held on Saturday afternoon. Lori traded shifts with Rita so she could go. Officer Trey Smith chose to sit with her. Lori tried to convince herself he was only there because Michah and he had become such good friends.

The weather was perfect for the outdoor ceremony. The amphitheater was packed with proud families and excited graduates. Lori's excitement was tempered by the knowledge that in just a little more than two weeks, Marcus and Michah would both be gone. She wondered if she would ever see either of them again.

Matthew had eyes on Lori. If he still had his daddy's knife, he could have taken her out. That rookie cop would not be a problem. At least that's what he kept telling himself as he sat three rows back, staring at the backs of their heads as they talked and laughed together. Truth was, he was scared. Matthew had never taken a life, and he couldn't rid himself of the truth he had grown up with. It wasn't up to him to decide who lived and who died. It wasn't up to Conrad Meyer, either.

"Michah, I don't know what to do. Or what to think. Marcus just keeps talking like we're going to Centerville together and . . . Why does he think that?" Lori was confused. Marcus was, for all intents and purposes, healed from the injuries he had suffered during the bank robbery.

Tim had healed too and was back to work. He was going to church regularly now. And Brenda knew without a doubt that he loved her passionately. He had even cleaned the gutters.

"There is definitely something off," Michah agreed. "He seems to think you've already agreed to go with him. You would go with him, marry him, if he asked you?"

At Lori's vehement nod, Michah spoke his thoughts. "Maybe I should try to talk to him again."

"Please," Lori requested. "Do you think he has forgotten that he didn't already talk to me about this?" she wondered out loud.

"Like the opposite of forgetting something that happened? Remembering something that didn't happen?" Michah grew quiet for a few moments. Looking sharply at Lori, he asked, "Have you noticed any other false memories?"

Hesitating thoughtfully, Lori asked him "Was it you or Marcus who told detective Mitchell the whole story about the Simpsons?"

"I did." Michah looked at Lori. Seeing the troubled look that flitted across her face, he added, "Marcus told you he told the detective the story." It wasn't a question. "Marcus and I need to have a long talk." Dropping some bills on the table, he walked out of The Diner.

"Hey, big brother! How's the packing coming?" He walked into the apartment and spotted his twin sitting at the small table staring vacantly off into space. "Marcus?"

"Lori doesn't want to go with me, does she?" He spoke softly, emotions clogging his throat.

"Yes. She does." Michah decided to just come right out and say it. "Why have you been just assuming she was going? And now you're assuming she isn't."

"I asked her to go. I asked her to marry me." Marcus hesitated before he finished his thought. "Now I think she's changed her mind."

"When, Marcus? When did you ask her?" Michah stared down his brother.

"While I was in the hospital. I told her I got the job and I asked her to go with me." Marcus was staring back at Michah, a puzzled look on his face.

Michah shook his head. "You told us you got the job. You told us. Then you passed out again. And the next time you woke up, Lori had left for work."

"Are you telling me I dreamed I asked her? I dreamed she said yes?"

"Just like you dreamed you told Detective Mitchell all about the Simpsons."

"That wasn't me either?" Marcus scrubbed a hand across his face.

"You better go talk to Lori," Michah told him. "Now, brother. She's only got two weeks to get ready for this," he added.

"It was so real. I really thought . . . ." He trailed off and continued to sit, staring at the table.

"Marcus! Get up! Go! Talk to Lori! *Now!*" Michah rose and planted a hand on each side of Marcus's folded ones. He stared at his twin, daring him not to get up and go.

Marcus rose and walked out the door. Michah watched him until he walked out of sight. He was headed for The Diner.

CHAPTER FOURTEEN

———†———

C*on found out we lost that knife.* Matthew Simpson fretted. *He's mad. He's really mad.* He paced the floor of his tiny efficiency apartment. He had been stuck there for days, not allowed to go anywhere, having takeout delivered to his door. It was getting expensive, and he was running out of money.

Boss will just get even madder if I leave, he thought to himself.

"I want to talk to Daddy, but boss says I can't go back to the cemetery. He didn't tell me that *before* I took those people out there and tied them up." Shaking his head, he continued to mutter. "It was such a good plan, tie those people up to Mama and Daddy's tombstone. They're gonna find out how mad I am as soon as they get smart enough to figure out the message." He snickered.

"Boss didn't say I couldn't kill two birds with one stone. I got them out of the way like he said. And I didn't kill them. And I made sure someone would find them. Boss didn't say it couldn't be that security guard." Simpson spoke to his reflection in the mirror. "Too bad it wasn't Mark," he continued.

"Since Con doesn't know his way around here like I do, I knew he was gonna let me decide our escape route. He's already said I can decide this time too." He rubbed his hands together gleefully. "This is so much fun! He won't stay mad," Matt assured himself.

Lori's shift had just ended when Marcus walked through the door. She heard the bell jingling and knew someone had come in, but she walked on back, through the kitchen, to the time clock.

As soon as she clocked out, she grabbed her purse from her locker and walked back to the dining area. She smiled and waved at a couple of coworkers as she pushed through the double doors. Marcus was standing, hesitantly, by the entrance. Lori could see he was nervous, panicked even.

"Hey, Marcus. How's the packing going?" Lori said the first thing that came to mind.

"We need to talk," he told her, not wanting to waste a moment on small talk or anything else. He held the door open and took her arm when they reached the sidewalk.

Lori let him hold her arm. Any touch from Marcus sent excited shivers up and down her spine. "What's wrong?" she asked.

"My brother tells me my memory of that day in the hospital is flawed." He stopped and held both of her arms gently. Staring down into her beautiful green eyes, he continued, "Lori, will you go to Illinois with me? Will you marry me? I thought I asked you when I was in the hospital, but Michah says I didn't," he rattled on.

Putting a hand to his lips, she answered him, a chuckle in her voice. "Yes, yes I will. I just wish you had asked me sooner because I'm not sure how I can be ready in two weeks."

Marcus looked at Lori. "Did you just say yes?" He felt certain his ears were deceiving him.

Grinning, Lori responded, "Yes. I said yes."

He pulled her in for a bear hug and told her, "I will help you. I will do all your packing for you. All you have to do is give notice for your job and get your family here for the wedding."

"Who's going to have time to plan a wedding? Will you do that too?" she asked him, still smiling broadly.

"Lori, I'm so sorry. I really messed up, didn't I? Can we plan the wedding for after we get to Chicago? That would give us more time. We could have it in my church."

"Don't you want Michah to marry us? I know I do." She looked up at him and saw the stress fleet across his face.

"He leaves the day after we leave," Marcus remembered.

She noted he had said *we* and was glad he wasn't doubting her willingness to go with him. "We leave on Monday, right?" Marcus had talked about it so much she had the itinerary memorized.

"Yes," he answered.

"Okay. I'll call my family and get them here. We will need to do blood tests and make a trip to the courthouse for the license. I'll give my notice, and I can pack my own stuff—there isn't much."

Marcus nodded as she spoke. "I did tell you the church has a parsonage, didn't I? We do have a place to live."

"Yes, you did. Did you tell them you were bringing a wife?" Lori rolled the word around in her mind. *Wife*. She liked the sound of it.

Shaking his head, he admitted he had not. "You seemed so hesitant to go. I didn't want to tell them and then have to embarrass myself my first day there by telling them you wouldn't come." Looking into those clear green eyes, he had to ask, "You really will come with me?"

"Yes, Marcus. Yes. I really will come with you." Pulling her close, he kissed her deeply. He didn't care that they were standing on the sidewalk with people walking by staring at them. Lori was going with him. That was the only thing important to him now.

Lori's hands shook as she called the familiar number on the cell phone the Boys had given her for Christmas. It had been almost nine months since she last talked to her family. She was grateful Detective Mitchell had so readily given her permission to talk to her family. He seemed to wonder why she hadn't before. Knowing Curtis had found her had changed everything; not all of it was bad.

"I'll get it!" Megan shouted when she heard her mother's phone ringing on the kitchen counter.

"Wrights. This is Megan," she began, not recognizing the strange area code.

"Hi, Megan." A breathless voice came through the phone.

"It's Lori!" Megan shouted when she heard her sister's voice. "Lori! Wow! Hi." Bubbling over with excitement, she could barely get sensible words out of her mouth. "How are you? What's going on?" Lori's little sister bubbled on.

Instant tears slid down Lori's cheeks when she heard her sister's voice across the miles. "Hey, Megs. I'm good. And it's really good to hear your voice. I've missed you so much."

Megan was crying too. Becky Wright stood beside her daughter Megan and waited, almost patiently, for Megan to hand her the phone. Silent tears were tracking down her face as well.

Keeping the conversation with her sister as brief as she could, she asked her to hand the phone to their mom. "I love you, Megan, and I'll be seeing you soon, but I really need to talk to mom now."

"Lori! Honey, is everything okay? Todd tries to keep us in the loop as much as possible with Maquire—Arnold—but there's a lot he can't tell us." Until that moment, it hadn't crossed Lori's mind that her family would already know Maquire was here in Tulsa. Apparently Detective Mitchell had talked to her brother months ago, after the fire.

"I'm okay, Mom." Fresh tears were falling and she heard a sob rip from her mother's throat. "I really am okay. In fact . . ." Lori told her mother about Marcus and his proposal and the wedding that was only a couple weeks away. "I know it's short notice, but . . ."

"Nonsense! Even if you were telling me this wedding was this afternoon, we would be there!" Becky Wright was smiling for the first time in months.

Hearing the smile in her mother's voice, Lori laughed, and her mother's smile got bigger. "We will be there," she informed her daughter.

After another twenty minutes of conversation with her mom, working on details and outlining plans, the two hung up. It was the first of many calls that would fly back and forth between Tulsa and Pittsburgh over the next two weeks.

And the two weeks flew by. Lori's family cleared their calendars. She and Marcus got their blood tests and their license. Lori packed her meager apartment and gave notice at The Diner. And she told the three people whose houses she cleaned.

Marcus called his new flock and filled them in on his wedding plans. Their excitement and joy at the prospect had him in tears. He knew he was going to love those people.

And Marcus took Lori to a small jewelry shop where the jewelry was all handmade locally. They picked out a set of wedding bands that had been hammered out of a recycled silver candlestick. They were inexpensive and very beautifully made. Lori loved them.

And Marcus loved Lori and prayed that one day soon, he would be able to give her a real diamond and a gold wedding band. Maybe not as big and fancy as the one he knew Mrs. Drake wore but still very beautiful.

On that last Sunday morning, Marcus, Michah, Lori and her family, Tonya and several of Lori's other friends from The Diner, and a few police officers and first responders who had become their friends trooped into the church together.

Matt paced the floor of his drab room. Meyer had told him to lay low for a few days. Then he had ordered him—*ordered him*—to go keep an eye on Lori again. He wanted to know everything she did, everywhere she went. Just how was he supposed to do that without getting caught? The girl had cops and twins surrounding her *all* the time. It wasn't safe for him to hang out at The Diner because Mark and Mike would make him. He settled for sitting at the bus stop or in his car or at the bar next door.

When he saw the big moving van with the fancy car in tow behind it pull up in front of her apartment building Friday evening, he didn't think too much of it. Somebody was moving. Lori didn't have a car, so it had nothing to do with her.

The moving van sat there all day Saturday. And on Sunday, when Lori and the Boys went to church, some people followed them in the fancy car from behind the moving van. Matt saw both cars pull into the church parking lot and kept going. He was hungry. He was going to The Diner for pancakes.

When he pulled up at The Diner he was surprised to get a spot right out front. Cops usually got that parking place. He pushed on the door and discovered it was locked. A small sign taped to the inside of the door at eye level finally caught his eye. It said simply, "Closed until 3 pm to cater a wedding." Grumbling to himself, Matt got back in his car and drove out to the interstate to the Waffle Shack for pancakes.

After breakfast the man got back in his car and turned the key, figuring he would be back at the church in time to see them all leave. He wondered where they would all go for lunch today since The Diner was closed.

Nothing happened. He turned the key again. Nothing again. Popping the hood, he got out and raised it to look inside. He had no idea what was wrong. His daddy could fix cars, but Matt never got the chance to learn from him. One more reason why he hated the twins.

He finally had to get a tow. He had his car dropped off at a shop close to his apartment. One man was there working on Sunday morning. He took Matt's keys and his contact information and told him they would call him the next day as soon as they figured out what was going on. He also told Matt he thought it was probably the starter.

Matt mumbled "Thanks" and headed toward his rooms. No way was he going to watch Lori today. Not on foot. He was going to watch the game this afternoon. He deserved a day off.

Pastor Victor gave a brief message and they all sang a few songs and prayed. The offering baskets were passed around.

Then Lori quietly slipped out of her seat and back to the women's lounge. Her mother and little sister, Megan, followed her. As they passed the kitchen, Lori smelled the most tantalizing aromas. Tonya was outdoing herself for this wedding party.

Thirty minutes later, strains of the wedding march filtered down the hallway. "It's time, honey," Becky Wright told her oldest daughter.

"Mom, I can't believe how perfectly your dress fits me." Lori hugged her mom again. "Thank you for bringing it."

"Just make sure she gets it back so I can wear it someday too!" Megan insisted vehemently.

The dress was modest. Her arms and shoulders peeped through delicate lace. The dress itself was snow-white satin. Beadwork covered the bodice and trimmed the neckline and wrists. A short train barely touched the floor and whispered behind her as she moved down the hallway to the end of the aisle. The veil touched her chin and a lacy cap was pinned in place atop her long, blond locks. Green eyes shimmered and her cheeks were pink with excitement.

She paused with her father at the end of the aisle. Squeezing her hand, Trenton Wright looked down at his eldest daughter and whispered in her ear, "Are you sure, sweetheart? You love Marcus?"

Looking down the aisle, seeing Marcus standing there waiting for her, she nodded. "Yes, Daddy, I'm sure."

"Then let's do this, honey." He tugged at her to remind her to walk. Her eyes never wavered from Marcus's eyes. His love for her shone through a damp haze of tears that occasionally escaped and slipped down his cheeks. Lori's beautiful green eyes shimmered with the bright tears that glistened like diamonds as they slid down her cheeks.

Lori had never been happier. Never. And looking at Marcus, she could tell he was happy too. His handsome face glowed. Dark brown eyes never left her face. The dimple stood out, never disappearing.

Michah read from the thirteenth chapter of First Corinthians. He spoke solemnly of the sanctity of marriage. They repeated their vows, their eyes never wavering from each other.

"I now pronounce you husband and wife," Michah said. "You may kiss the bride." And with that, Marcus put his arms around Lori and drew her close. Cupping her chin in his hand, he took her lips and kissed her so tenderly Lori's knees went weak. She had no doubts about his love for her. None.

Family and friends gathered in the dining hall behind the church for the reception. Tonya had truly outdone herself. And the whole crew from The Diner had chipped in on a wedding cake, and now they pitched in to help Tonya serve the meal.

The afternoon flew by in a whirlwind of laughter, hugs, kisses, and good-byes. Marcus never left Lori's side and Michah was always nearby too. By 3:00 Tonya was gone, along with two of the other waitresses, to open The Diner. By five the dining hall was empty and spotless.

Mr. and Mrs. Drake, along with Tim and Brenda, had gifted Lori and Marcus with a night in a very nice hotel room. They checked into their "honeymoon suite," as it were, at six. The next twelve hours were theirs, and theirs alone.

CHAPTER FIFTEEN

———————†———————

Conrad Meyer glanced casually at the young couple checking out of the hotel on Monday morning. He was sitting in his favorite seat near the entrance to the dining room. He choked on his coffee and quickly covered his mouth with his linen napkin to keep his coughs to himself. What were Lori and that twin doing here? And why were they so happy and lovey-dovey?

By seven Monday morning the families—the Stouts and Wrights—had gathered for a send-off breakfast at The Diner. More tearful good-byes were said. Lori looked around the room at all the familiar faces—people she had come to love and call family, for they were much closer and dearer than friends.

Mr. Tam came up to the newlyweds and shook Marcus's hand and gave Lori a side hug. "You two be happy together," he told them. He handed Lori a sealed envelope with a greeting card inside and walked away, pushing open the door and stepping onto the sidewalk as he snugged his hat down on his head.

After the newlyweds had left for the hotel on Sunday, Michah, Todd, Pastor Victor, and several other men from the church had loaded the moving van with everything from Lori's apartment. Then they had driven over to load up everything at Marcus and Michah's apartment.

The car was packed. Stuffed, more like it. It was hooked to a tow dolly being pulled by a medium-size moving van. Lori's family had paid for the moving vehicles as their wedding gift. And unbeknownst to Lori and Marcus, when the church members had gotten together and loaded Lori and Marcus's belongings from their apartments, they had also given them just about everything they could possibly need to set up housekeeping. There was even a six-foot artificial Christmas tree buried in the load somewhere.

Lori's mom had spent a week furiously packing up everything in their home in Pennsylvania that belonged to Lori. As she worked, an idea had formed. A quick phone call to her son, Todd, who had the connections, had put that plan into action. That's what prompted the moving van rental.

Later that morning more tears were shed and more good-byes were said. Michah clung to his twin and his new sister tightly. Tears rolled unchecked down all three faces. "Be safe, little brother," Marcus told him. "And know that your home is with us whenever you want it."

Lori nodded her agreement and hugged him again. "Thank you, Michah, for being a best friend to me when I didn't know how badly I needed one."

"You're welcome, little sister." He grinned down at her. "You keep my big brother out of trouble for me, okay?"

A very angry Conrad Meyer had discreetly followed the couple to The Diner and waited for them to reappear on the sidewalk outside. Simpson had no idea how much trouble he was in!

"It is your starter, Mr. Simpson." The mechanic had called Matt at nine on Monday morning. He was still sleeping off the alcohol buzz from his day off. "We can have it ready late this afternoon," he was told.

"Good, good," Matt said, and it was decided that he would pick his car up at 4:00. Then the day got interesting.

"Simpson!" Conrad Meyer barked at his hired stooge. "What's going on with Lori these days? I haven't had an update for a while." He had good reason to believe Simpson wasn't doing a very good job.

"Same old, same old, boss. She works and goes to church and hangs out with those twin guys," Simpson told him. "Then she does it all again the next day."

"Where were you this morning when the moving van left?" Meyer cornered Simpson.

"I hadn't gotten there yet." Simpson knew better than to lie about that. "That van had nothing to do with her. Some people with a fancy car were there visiting a couple of days on their way to wherever they were headed." He assumed as much.

"Those people with the fancy car were Lori's parents and that detective brother of hers," he barked, grinding his teeth when he mentioned Todd. "They left early this morning. And Lori was driving one of the twins' cars while one of the twins was driving the van and towing the other car!" Meyer was in a rage by now and screaming at Simpson.

"Boss, I'm sorry. The starter went out on my car yesterday. They couldn't fix it till today." Matt knew he better come clean. As it was, he was in fear of his life. "It'll be ready this afternoon."

"If you had said something, I could have put Steve on her for a while. Or I could have gotten you a loaner car so you could *stay on her* like I told you to!"

Matt gulped and tried to breathe. Boss was really mad, and this was bad. *Lori moved? And he missed that?*

"As soon as I get my car back, I'll go to The Diner and find out where she went," he assured Conrad.

"You better find her. And you better find her *fast*." Matt started to reply but realized the line was dead. His boss had hung up on him.

He was so stupid. Why did he think he could get away with not watching Lori? He should have known Meyer was gonna be watching him.

The only time Charles Arnold, aka Conrad Meyer, could ever remember being this mad before was when Lori had skipped out on him in Pittsburgh. He would kill Simpson as soon as his usefulness ran out. Right now, he had bigger problems to solve.

The plan had been to use Simpson's car for the next robbery. Simpson's—and his car's—usefulness would expire then. Both could disappear. Now Simpson's car needed to disappear until the robbery. Even then, the mechanic would probably remember working on it and turn the lead in to the authorities.

Arnold decided to just let the authorities take care of Simpson for him. And Charles figured even though the man was pretty dumb, he was smart enough to stay out of sight for a while. Steve had already located another car for the last robbery. They would use it this time instead. Steve's usefulness had not expired.

Matthew Simpson buried his head in the menu at The Diner later that evening. Believing the twins and Lori were gone, he had thrown caution to the wind and sat at a table in the middle of the room. He wanted to be able to hear as many of the conversations going on around him as possible. He needed to find Lori fast.

Imagine his surprise when the door opened as the waitress was bringing him his water and the menu, and Michah Stout walked in. *Didn't the boss say the twins moved? Well, they must not have moved very far.*

Michah ordered a burger with the works, fries, and sweet tea. Then he added apple pie for dessert. He was splurging, he knew, but this was the last meal he would ever eat at The Diner.

He watched the other diners reflected in the mirror in front of him as he ran through his mental checklist and made sure he was on track to leave in the morning. He had handed over the keys to the landlord and was spending a second night on Trey's sofa. Trey would take him to the airport in the morning. His packed bags were already sitting in a corner at Trey's apartment.

Conversations swirled around him. Mr. Tam stood beside him briefly to wish him well. "Have you heard from Lori and Marcus?" he wanted to know.

"Marcus called me from a rest stop north of Springfield, Illinois, a couple hours ago," Michah shared with him. "They should make it to Centerville before dark," he added.

Mr. Tam nodded and mumbled a few words of encouragement and blessings before he shuffled over to his usual table and righted his cup. A waitress appeared to fill it for him and take his order.

Michah stared into the mirror watching the diners behind him. He wanted to carry this scene, this place, with him always. This town, this diner, had been home to him for a very long time. These people—Mr. Tam, Tonya, Rita, Trey, Pastor Victor, Tim, and Brenda—had become his friends and his family. He would miss them all. A lot.

He eyed the DVD laying on the counter beside him. Trey had given it to him when he dropped him off at The Diner. He had said it was "just something to remember them by." Michah wondered what it was. He also wondered who the man was who was sitting at the table in the middle of the room. There was something familiar about him, something very familiar.

Michah finished his meal and said good-bye to his friends, getting a hug from both Tonya and Rita. When he went to shake Mr. Tam's hand, the man stood up and wrapped his bony arms around Michah and gave him what, Michah was sure, was meant to be a bear hug. He walked out the door brushing a wave of tears from his eyes.

So Lori and Mark had moved to Centerville, Illinois? Matt was excited. Finding Lori had been much easier than he had expected. He finished his meal and left The Diner shortly after Michah. *I hope Mike didn't recognize me*, he thought to himself as he settled into the driver's seat of his new ride. The boss had gotten it for him; he would be driving it for the next robbery.

As soon as he got back to the hotel, he called Conrad. "Hey, boss," he greeted the man he knew only as Conrad Meyer. "That Lori chick and Mark moved to Centerville, Illinois. Mike is still in town, but he's leaving for South America in the morning." Matt was feeling pretty proud of himself for all the information he had gathered today.

Charles Arnold, aka Conrad Meyer, aka Cameron Nash, aka Curtis Maquire, merely grunted a response and hung up on him. "Okay."

"That's the thanks I get?" Simpson spoke into the dead phone line.

"Sorry, sweetheart. Business. I had to take the call." Meyer rubbed his girlfriend's bare arms as he pulled her in for a smooch and watched the goings-on across the street at the bank. *Good*, the man thought to himself. *Centerville is close enough to Chicago I can make it work.*

CHAPTER SIXTEEN

———†———

The next Sunday, Marcus preached his first sermon. He had already met most of the congregation. They had all turned out to help unload the van, unpack the boxes, and keep them all fed while they worked.

Marcus felt like he had come home. His first sermon reflected it. "Everyone has heard the story of the prodigal son, yes?" he began. "Well, I may have never been here before physically, but I feel as though I have always belonged here."

Two weeks later, Lori was still going through boxes and putting her new home in order. She loved it here. She loved the people she was getting to know. She loved being the pastor's wife.

She was still afraid of Curtis or one of his goons finding them again. Detective Mitchell had been happy to let Lori leave Oklahoma. His only condition was that he give law enforcement at her new home a heads-up and that she pay them a visit soon after their arrival in town. He did, and she had.

She opened up the last box her mother had packed from home. Shoe boxes full of party shoes. And a few small handbags to match. She had no idea what she would do with them now but dutifully decided to store them in the closet in the smallest of the three bedrooms. For now that room was being used for storage.

Without really thinking about it, she opened up each purse for a quick peek inside. "Aha! That's what happened to you!" She had finally found her favorite lip gloss. Another purse had a fifty-dollar bill tucked down in the corner. "Groceries! Yeah!" she chuckled as she tried to remember what had prompted her to stash fifty bucks. *Out of sight and out of mind.* She honestly had no idea why she had ever thought that way. It seemed so immature. Still chuckling, she reminded herself that she had been very immature when she was partying with Curtis. *And that was less than a year ago? Incredible!* she thought to herself and chuckled again.

The last purse had a wadded-up gum wrapper in the bottom of it. And it was wrapped around a chewed piece of gum. Curtis was always chewing gum and then just throwing it out the window or on the sidewalk. Once he even stuck a piece under the table in a fancy restaurant he had taken her to.

A light bulb went on. Lori reached for her cell phone and called Detective Snyder. The man was Lori's Centerville contact and a member of Faith Unfolding Chapel. "Detective Snyder? This is Lori Wright. Stout." She loved her new name but still fumbled with using it to introduce herself. She was able to remind herself before she wrote it down, but not so in conversation.

"Yes, Mrs. Stout. Is everything all right? What can I do for you?" Detective Snyder really liked and respected the Stouts. Pastor and Lori were rapidly wending their way into the hearts of the members of Faith Unfolding.

Lori hurried through a brief explanation of what she had been doing and what she found. "I'm positive this is Curtis's gum. I remember he was about to toss it out the window when I stopped him and made him put it in the wrapper. He laughed at me and then told me I could not leave it in the car. So I put it in my purse and then forgot all about it. Curtis always had gum in his mouth. He said he had problems with his ears because of his sinuses, and chewing gum kept his ears from being stuffed up," Lori told him.

"He used to take me to all these fancy restaurants and then stick his wad of gum under the table." Shaking her head, she added, "So embarrassing."

The detective was barely able to tamp down his excitement. Maybe this was the break they needed. They had all kinds of DNA but no way to match it to anyone. "I'll send an officer over to collect it right away, Mrs. Stout. This could be a big break for us or it could send us back to square one. Either way, it's more than we had this morning."

As soon as Detective Snyder ended his conversation with Lori, he set up a conference call between himself, Detective Mitchell, and Lori's brother, Detective Wright. "We may finally have a break," he told the two long distance.

After about twenty minutes of conversation and tossing thoughts around, Snyder and Wright both agreed they would be on the next flight out to Tulsa. Snyder was bringing the DNA evidence with him.

"As much as I'd love to see my sister," Wright said, "you've got the bulk of the evidence there, Mitchell. We'll meet there."

Snyder arranged for his flight, hurried home to pack a bag, and stopped by Pastor and Lori Stout's home to pick up the gum. She unceremoniously dropped it in the evidence bag he held out for her. "Maybe now we can finally put an end to this mess," Lori commented and released a deep breath.

"You're not the only one who hopes so," Snyder responded. "Never doubt for a minute, we will get them. And we will get them solid. They'll do some real prison time," he told her.

Later that afternoon, the three men sat in the conference room at Mitchell's station pouring over notes. Mitchell spoke up to say, "I followed up on all the names the Stout boys gave me from Simpson's old church. Neither of the Simpson boys have ever been arrested. One of the boys that was in that Tuesday night class is doing time. I paid him a visit last weekend. He said he had no idea what ever happened to the Simpsons and didn't care. He also told me he had never heard of Charles Arnold or Curtis Maquire. I think I believe him. He's in for rape and drunk driving. Had some illegal smoke on him too. Not enough to bust him for intent to sell."

The two detectives nodded their agreement as he continued, "I dug pretty deep and found no reason to believe the two had ever crossed paths."

"I'm concerned a jury will call our gum circumstantial evidence. Arnold can probably afford a good lawyer to spin that for him." Todd Wright spoke up..

"Which is why I'm sticking around this one-horse town for a couple of weeks," Snyder chimed in. "It's a long shot, but he may still be here. And if he likes high-priced restaurants, maybe I can catch him sticking gum under his table." Both men stared at him incredulously.

"That is such a long shot." Mitchell stated the obvious.

"Why you? Your department doesn't even have him for a crime? Why would they let you do that?" Todd asked.

"They wouldn't. I am on vacation"—Snyder glanced at his watch—"as of six hours ago. And for two weeks."

"How does your family feel about you spending your vacation working someone else's case?" Mitchell wanted to know. That would have started a huge fight in his house. His wife was very protective of his "down time."

"I'm single," he said and shrugged. "No one around to care."

Todd knew that feeling. He knew his parents and his sisters cared. He also knew he didn't take vacations because he didn't like being by himself all the time. And two weeks alone? That was thirteen days too many. "What makes you think he's still around?" he asked Detective Snyder.

"How many banks did he hit in Pittsburgh?" Snyder answered his own question: "Five."

"Yeah, if the two that happened after Lori left town were really his work," Todd chimed in. "And before he came to Pittsburgh, we think he was responsible for five robberies in Boston," he added.

"Tulsa has only seen three robberies that look like his work." Mitchell nodded. "You could be right, Snyder."

"So where should I eat tonight?"

The three men talked well into the evening. Snyder ended up at a little Italian joint that didn't really look like much from the outside, but everybody who was anybody could be seen there. And it didn't require a reservation.

The officers on duty that evening were asked to make the rounds of all the hotels and motels again with Charles Arnold's photo.

Mitchell strode past the front desk and headed straight back to his office the next morning, a sense of purpose in his stride. Arnold was still there. He was staying at a small hotel on the south side of the city, near the interstate.

"He's registered under the name Conrad Meyer." Mitchell had called Snyder and Wright in for a conference before he even had his first cup of coffee. Now he brought the other detectives up to speed.

"My guess is he's going to hit somewhere north of the city next," Todd commented. "If and when he hits near where he's staying, it'll be number five."

"Clue me in on some good restaurants that are close to the banks up that way. Maybe that's how he scopes them out," Snyder said.

"Hey, Wright, get your team back east to try to find some camera footage of Arnold doing his fancy dining thing so we can get a better read on how he makes his plans," Mitchell requested.

"Already been done. My sister gave me a list of his favorite restaurants last night. She's supposed to call me as soon as she remembers when they ate there and if she missed any." Todd and Lori were making up for lost time now and talked every day. He knew she talked to their parents daily too.

"It was so long ago I doubt we'll get camera footage, but someone might remember seeing them." They all knew most businesses only keep their surveillance footage a few days.

"So let's get his picture out to the restaurants nearest the banks north of town and have the management watch for him." Mitchell picked up the phone and made it happen.

"I'm gonna make a reservation for tonight." Snyder grinned and stepped over to the corner of the room to make his call.

Detective Wright called Detective Mitchell the next morning. "Lori called me last night with a partial list of the dates they ate at those restaurants. There were two lunches and two evening meals right across the street within days of the robbery that Lori was supposed to drive for."

An hour later both Detective Wright and Detective Snyder joined Detective Mitchell in his office. "We're getting closer." Mitchell spoke with a hint of barely contained excitement in his voice.

"How does a cop from Chicago afford to eat in a fancy restaurant every night?" Todd teased Snyder four days later. The three detectives had not only developed an excellent working relationship, they had bonded in a deep Christian relationship as well. They were a team now. They were brothers now too.

"I don't have a family to feed." He shrugged and hid his moment of sadness by glancing at his phone. "And I live in the house I grew up in, which is paid for, so no rent or house payment."

"Maybe I should move back in with my folks." Todd chuckled.

Detective Mitchell's phone rang and the banter came to a halt as the three men listened to the conversation Mitchell put on speakerphone. "He's been spotted at five of the six restaurants on your list, detective Mitchell," the officer on desk duty informed him.

"Officer Batts also found out he has a reservation at eight tonight at Rickie's," the man said. He went on to add, "Well, we think it's him. He's using a different alias this time. But the hostess says Mark Stout is a new name and it's unusual for someone new to visit for the first time on a weeknight."

The conversation ended and the three men stared at each other. "What's the purpose of using Marcus's name?" Todd wanted to know.

"Now I'm wondering just how many other aliases the man has used." Mitchell voiced his thoughts.

"I need to make a reservation." Snyder strode out of the room.

Rickie's was a busy place. Detective Snyder ordered broiled salmon, a baked potato, and the house salad. "And keep my glass of tea full, please," he told his waitress. She nodded and smiled politely before she walked away to turn in his order.

Detective Derrick Snyder sat quietly at his back-corner table and looked discreetly around the restaurant. He had requested an out-of-the-way table when he made his reservation, explaining that he wasn't comfortable sitting out in the middle alone. He had actually chuckled and told the woman who took his reservation that he didn't like women hitting on him while he tried to eat in peace. She had apparently bought it, because this was the perfect place to view the whole restaurant without drawing any attention.

Until his salad arrived, he pretended to play with his phone. All the while, he surreptitiously watched his fellow diners. When a lone man entered the restaurant and was seated near the front window, he nearly choked on his salmon. It was Charles Arnold. He sent a quick group text to the team that was spread out over a several-block radius: "He's here."

Snyder's waitress chose that moment to refill his iced tea, so he lost visual for a few seconds. When he was able to look again, Arnold was on his feet warmly greeting a curvaceous blond. He eyed them discreetly until their salads arrived.

He had ordered dessert, and the sugary concoction arrived shortly before their salads. He turned on the camera feature on his phone and toyed with it, pretending he wasn't sure how to use it. When Arnold took out his gum and stuck it under the table, he snapped a picture. Then he snapped a couple more of himself and his dessert just to make it look like he really didn't know how to use his camera.

After forcing himself to eat a few bites of his dessert, he asked for his check. Once he paid up, he left the restaurant.

An hour later, Arnold and his lady friend left the building and a well-hidden tail followed them. The woman drove and they went to the theater. Detective Snyder walked back into the restaurant and flashed his badge as he asked permission to retrieve the gum from under Charles Arnold's table.

"The DNA is a match for both wads of gum," Mitchell told the two detectives, Snyder and Wright. Todd had returned to Pittsburgh within the week of his trip to Oklahoma. Even offering to pay his own way hadn't netted him permission to continue working the case after it left his jurisdiction. Snyder had four days left of his vacation and then he had to return to Centerville.

Conference calls kept Lori's brother up to date, and he shared anything his department discovered as well. "We're still missing something," he said on this Tuesday morning. "Lori said something last night that got me thinking, though. She mentioned seeing Curtis – Charles Arnold - with another woman about a week before she left town. When she questioned him about it, he told her she was a client from the bank he was working with. He said he really had to 'lay on the charm and schmooze her good.'"

"Who do you think she really was?" Snyder wanted to know.

"We're working on figuring that out right now," Todd said. "I've sent a couple of blues out to talk to all the female employees at that bank. Hopefully we'll learn something this time." He added that the interviews that had taken place the morning after the robbery hadn't turned up anything useful.

CHAPTER SEVENTEEN

———————†———————

Snyder flew back to Chicago and drove home to Centerville Saturday afternoon. Sunday morning, he was in his seat at Faith Unfolding Chapel. He had really enjoyed the first couple of sermons Pastor Marcus Stout had preached. He was looking forward to hearing another one.

Early on Monday morning, Detective Wright entered the bank that had been robbed six weeks after his sister Lori had been flown away from Pittsburgh and the danger Charles Arnold had put her in.

When nothing new had been revealed by talking to the female employees at the bank where Lori was supposed to pick Arnold up, he decided it was possible the man had already begun working on plans for the next bank.

Flashing his badge at the guard standing just inside the glass entry doors, he explained his purpose for being there. "We have new information and we need to run it by your female employees," he stated simply.

The guard snapped to attention and keyed his shoulder microphone, asking for the bank president's response.

Within five minutes, Todd was seated in the president's office awaiting the entry of the first female employee. An hour later, and no nearer an answer, Todd thanked the man for his time and headed back toward the door.

"Detective?" A young teller touched his sleeve. *Sally?* He was pretty sure that was her name. "I just remembered something. Maybe it will help."

Sally proceeded to tell him that she finally remembered why she thought Arnold's face was familiar. "The woman from the library brought in a deposit a couple days before the robbery. Charles Arnold was the man with her. And I only remembered because you were pressing so hard about a woman helping him." The young woman spoke quickly. She was shaking, from fear, nervousness, excitement, or all three, Detective Wright wasn't sure. "I'm sorry I didn't think of it sooner," she apologized.

Grasping her arm and giving it a gentle squeeze, he thanked her. "You thought of it now. And you told me now. Thank you."

Heading for the door, he thought to walk back toward her and double check. "You do mean the library next door? Right?"

Her nod of affirmation sent him rushing out the doors and onto the busy sidewalk. It made sense. The library was the perfect location for casing the bank. Especially since there were very few restaurants nearby.

He was greeted at the front desk by a pixie of a woman. Short, dark brown hair framed a freckled face with dark brown eyes. Thick, black eyelashes fluttered coyly, and Todd realized the woman wore no makeup. It seemed a bit unusual but refreshing too. Her name tag said she was Ellen.

Flashing his badge, Todd got right to the point. Pulling Arnold's picture from his pocket, he asked, "Ellen? Do you know this man?"

Her pale face went paler and then blushed pink. Nodding, she responded, "Yes. That's Cam. Cameron Nash." Cocking her head to the side, she continued, "He grew a beard while we were dating. And he must be wearing colored contacts because his eyes were different too." She placed a protective hand on her stomach.

"Do you know where he is? How I can find him?" the detective wanted to know. Todd could barely hide his excitement at discovering another alias.

"No. I don't. He vanished into thin air last fall." Heaving a sigh, she appeared to be getting some emotions under control before she continued. "What did he do? Why are you looking for him?" she wanted to know.

"I need to talk to him. I have some questions for him about some bank robberies in the area." He gave the simple answer.

"I wish I did know where he was," the woman said, heaving another heavy sigh. When she rubbed her stomach again, Todd realized she was pregnant. And he thanked God Lori had a higher standard of morals.

Not wanting to be judgmental, he chose to ignore the protruding abdomen and ask the woman a few more questions. "Do you know which banks he was working for while he was in the area?" From what the detectives had managed to learn from Lori, Charles told the women he worked for the banking industry. His specific roll or job title was unclear.

"The one next door," she answered readily. "We met because he was early for an appointment and came in to make some copies he needed."

The detective nodded but kept silent. He felt this woman would talk plenty without encouragement.

"He was such a nice man. So handsome. We had a lot in common too," she continued, and rubbed her stomach again.

"Really?" Todd asked. "What sort of things do you like to do when you're not working?" Laughing at his own silliness, he added, "I'll bet you like to do all kinds of really noisy stuff—rock concerts and target shooting, maybe?"

Giggling and shaking her head, she answered him. "No, none of that. I bowl on a league across town at Bowl Haven. I guess that gets pretty noisy, though . . ." She trailed off.

Todd's thoughts shifted when she mentioned the bowling alley. It was right across the street from the fifth and final bank that was hit in Pittsburgh! "So he went bowling with you?"

"Yeah. And we went to the movies a couple times. You know, that old theater that shows all those old movies all the time?" she volunteered.

"You mean the one right there by the bowling alley?" he asked. At her nod of affirmation, he asked another question: "Did he take you to that burger joint . . . what's it called? Or was it tacos at the Mexican Hat?"

Not seeming to remember the name of the burger joint, she just nodded "Yes, that's where we ate."

Getting a faraway look in her eyes, she continued. "Sometimes I would cook something at my place and we would hang out there." After a thoughtful pause, she said, "Mostly we ate out."

A few minutes later, Todd had determined he had all the information she could give him, and giving her his card, he encouraged her to call him if she heard from Cameron Nash, or thought of anything else.

He almost added that she should call him if she wanted company at one of those old movies. She was so cute and tiny. Even with a baby bump.

He sat in his car and set up a conference call with Mitchell and Snyder. "Snyder, go see Lori. Ask her if she or Marcus ever saw anyone who even remotely resembled Arnold in The Diner. Mitchell, you check it out on your end," he suggested after briefing the other two detectives on his conversation with the pregnant woman.

Two days later the three connected on a conference call again. "I took a picture of Arnold to The Diner and showed everyone there," Mitchell told the other two detectives. "No one had ever seen him."

"Yeah, I can't imagine him showing up there. Lori would know him instantly." Todd had been certain. "We've been playing phone tag and I haven't gotten to talk to her since before our last conference call," he added.

"Well, then you will be glad to hear I caught up with her and Pastor Marcus this morning," Detective Snyder chimed in. "Arnold was apparently never in The Diner, but one of the Simpson men was there a lot. Simpson as in tombstone Simpson," he clarified.

Mitchell and Wright listened as Snyder unfolded the story of how he had gotten the information. "Pastor Marcus got a phone call from Michah late yesterday. It's the first time they've heard from him and he told them to send a friend request to his friend Officer Trey Smith on Facebook. Apparently Officer Smith had given him some video clips from The Diner and Michah had only just had a chance to look at them.

"All of their friends had been secretly working on them for several weeks because they wanted to surprise him with all the memories after he left for the missions job they knew he would soon have," Snyder told them by way of explanation. "Smith gave them to Michah after the wedding. Michah packed them away and forgot them till now.

"Michah thought one of the men in the background of several of the clips looked familiar and even suggested it might be Matthew Simpson. They sent the friend request immediately and Smith accepted within the hour." Snyder's growing excitement was palpable over the phone lines. "Pastor Marcus agrees with his brother — it's Simpson."

"You think he was surveilling for Arnold?" Detective Wright asked.

"It would explain the connection to the tombstone," Snyder pointed out. "Pastor Marcus recalled Matthew Simpson being particularly angry with Michah and him after his dad was arrested. He threatened the twins, told them he would get even and they would wish they had never told."

"Wait! The twins never told," Todd pointed out. "The men of the church figured it out after that flood, didn't they?" It was a rhetorical question. All three men knew the whole story. Weeks ago they had pulled the files and scoured them looking for anything to connect that crime to the tombstone and the current crimes.

"Why now? All these years later?" Snyder wondered.

"Simpson isn't the brightest crayon in the box," Mitchell explained. "He probably hadn't been able to figure out how to get even until Arnold approached him. Plus, both families have moved several times since then. Simpson probably lost track of them when they were still kids and only just managed to relocate them."

All three detectives agreed; it made sense in a somewhat disjointed and very twisted way.

"Now we just have to prove it." Todd spoke into the thoughtful silence on the phone.

"I'll get in touch with Officer Smith. He may have more clips that weren't included in what he gave Michah." Mitchell took a deep breath and let it out in a puff. "Even if he doesn't, we need to talk."

"I went back to the library yesterday to talk to Ellen again and was told she had her baby," Todd said. "So I went to the hospital and saw them both." Mitchell and Snyder listened, waiting to hear what else Detective Wright had learned from her. "She looks just like her mother . . . a tiny little doll." There was a faraway note in his voice.

"What else did you find out from her?" Snyder wanted to know.

Pulled back from his visions of two adorable pixies, Todd responded, "Huh? Oh. Nothing. She didn't know anything else." He seemed somewhat befuddled.

Mitchell chuckled. "So Detective, which 'doll' has you so totally discombobulated?"

Glad this was a conference call, Todd felt his cheeks go red. How had this woman he didn't even know gotten under his skin so easily? Worse yet, he adored that tiny baby girl of hers. Hers and Charles Arnold's!

"Someone needs to go back to The Diner and hang out under-cover and see if Simpson shows up again. We could tail him and figure out what Arnold's up to next." Mitchell spoke his thoughts out loud. "I'll get a couple of young blues on it. They've got a good chance of blending in with the kids from the seminary."

"How's the tail on Arnold working out?" Snyder wanted to know. All three men had been certain that any tail would be quickly made by Charles Arnold.

"It's not," Mitchell admitted. "We called it right when we decided it wouldn't work. Arnold drove in circles for almost an hour before our undercover blue gave up." Mitchell shook his head.

"I'm guessing following Simpson around will be a whole lot easier," Detective Wright decided. All three men were in agree-ment on that.

Officer Shelley Parker and Officer James Batts showed up at The Diner, arm in arm, laughing and carrying on like the college kids they were supposed to be. They even had books, borrowed from the seminary book store. They were on their first undercover assignment, and even though it was a relatively easy job, they both had plans to rock it and use it to help them climb the force's pro-motion ladder.

Taking a couple of selfies with Jim, Officer Parker surrepti-tiously eyed the other diners. Judging by the conversations and the friendly banter going on between the waitstaff and the customers, she decided everyone there was a regular. No one who looked like

Simpson or Arnold was there. Two weeks later, their assignment ended. Neither man had made an appearance.

Another couple of officers had been put undercover to work the businesses across the street from the bank Detective Mitchell thought they would hit next. It worked. Charles Arnold showed up late in the afternoon at an art gallery. When the business closed at nine that evening, he was still inside, hiding somewhere.

"Detective Mitchell? Sergeant Mason here." It was Mason's job to act as liaison between his blues and Detective Mitchell. "One of my undercovers saw Arnold enter the Famous Art Gallery. The other two who followed up swear he never left. He is still inside, apparently hiding somewhere." After a brief pause, he asked the detective, "Tonight the night?"

"Could be," Mitchell replied, adding, "Keep your team in place and on high alert. I'll notify SWAT.

Hanging up the phone, he made a quick call to the SWAT team leader to put them on alert. Then he took a moment to call Snyder and Wright. "Looks like we might be in business tonight," he told them. "Arnold is still inside the art gallery across the street from the bank."

"Keep us posted," Todd told him.

"Good luck! Catch them this time," Derrick Snyder requested.

Charles Arnold wandered casually around the art gallery. He knew he'd been made. He knew he had been tailed there. He could feel eyes on him as he tried to look interested in some of the ugliest paintings he had ever seen.

His mind was working hard, trying to decide the best course of action, when he found himself standing beside the employee break room. The men's room was right beside the doorway, so he slipped in there for a moment.

Staring at himself in the mirror, Charles raised a hand and scrubbed it down his jaw and around the back of his neck. What to do? What to do? A plan began to form. When the door opened, his eyes rested briefly, in the mirror, on an undercover cop. At least the man looked like an undercover cop. As soon as he went into the stall, Charles slipped out the door and quickly entered the employee break room.

Lockers along the wall to his left caught his eye, and finding most weren't locked, he used the tail of his shirt like a glove and started opening them, searching for anything he thought would be useful. Quickly, quietly, keeping a wary eye on the door, he gathered the items he thought might be useful and then locked himself in the employee restroom.

First he donned a maintenance jumpsuit with the name "Wade" embroidered on the chest. One of the female employees had left a wig in her locker. Charles put it on. The long, blond trusses made him chuckle. A ball cap and a pair of work gloves completed the ensemble. It was 9:00.

Recalling an exit to the alley just down the hall, he grabbed the trash bag full of discarded drink cups and takeout containers and casually opened the break room door. Hearing voices heading his way but seeing no one, he walked quickly toward the exit.

Once he made it out the door and into the alley, he tossed the bag in the dumpster and kept walking down the alley, getting out of his disguise as he went. The jumpsuit went in the dumpster behind an insurance office. The ball cap was two doors down at the real estate office. And the wig was dumped behind the dance academy.

CHAPTER EIGHTEEN

———————†———————

I t was four miles to his hotel. Arnold walked. As he walked, he thought through his new plan. He quickly decided to leave Steve and Matt in the dark. They would show up at one in the morning to rob the bank with him, and he would never show up. They might get arrested. Charles didn't care.

When he got to his hotel, he packed his bags and called a cab. He was going to Chicago to take care of some unfinished business.

The cab driver dropped him off at the airport. Figuring getting a flight at this late hour would be something the ticket agent would remember, he hung around until the next flight arrived and then headed for the car rental business, trying to blend in with the other disembarking passengers who would be renting a vehicle. While he waited, he dug through his carry-on and found his new identity. He would be Craig Adams.

An hour later, he pulled through the drive-through of an all-night burger joint and got himself some food. He had just gotten back on the highway when his phone rang. A glance told him it was Steve. He chose not to answer it.

"Hey, Con! Where are you?" Steve asked, remembering to use his boss's current alias. A few seconds later he added, "Not sure what to do at this point. If I don't hear from you in half an hour, I'm outta here."

Noting a sign for a rest stop a half mile ahead, Charles swung in. He was going to get rid of this phone. While he was at it, he would eliminate the car's built-in tracking. He'd watched Steve do it several times now; it would be a piece of cake.

Finding a spot that was as far as possible from the semi trucks that were parked there for the night, their drivers sleeping in the built-in bunks, he got out and took a moment to stretch his legs and look around.

Pulling the phone from his pocket, he pulled out the SIM card and the battery, and then, after wiping the phone clean with a left-over napkin, he stomped on it before using the napkin to pick it up and throw it away. Then he disabled the car's tracking.

After shuffling off to the comfort station and buying himself a cup of really bad coffee, he was back on the road again. Stuffing a stick of gum in his mouth and putting the wrapper in his food bag, he decided he was pretty proud of himself. He had played it pretty smart, he thought, not dumping his trash from a Tulsa fast food joint in an eastbound rest stop trash can an hour out of Tulsa.

"Sergeant, we've got a possible suspect sitting on the curb near the rear entrance to the bank. He's dressed all in black with a large, black backpack that looks empty." One of the blues spoke softly into his shoulder mic. Several police officers were hidden in the near vicinity.

"Watch him" was all Mason said in response.

"I've got eyes on a dark sedan parked around the corner from the dance studio," another officer reported. "Could be nothing, but the license plate has been obscured and I haven't gotten close enough to make it out. I will, though. Someone is inside the vehicle."

Ten minutes went by before Mason got his next report. "Sergeant, I got a read on the plate." The officer read off the plate, and Mason typed the info into his onboard computer.

"Officer Batts, the car is stolen," Mason said quietly into his shoulder mic. "Get some backup and then arrest the perp."

Feeling certain that this was supposed to be the getaway car, Mason called Detective Mitchell and filled him in.

"Is Arnold still holed up in the art gallery?" the detective wanted to know. "Because if he is, you might want to wait for him to come out before you take out the getaway car," he suggested. "You don't want to tip him off. We need him out of business."

Mason hustled to tell his men to stand down and wait for Charles Arnold to make an appearance. "Keep eyes on that car. Keep eyes on the curb-sitter. If it looks like the car is leaving the area, tail it and then arrest the driver."

"Con, it's 1:30. I'm outta here." Steve stood up, shouldered his empty backpack, and headed for the spot where Matt was supposed to be parked and waiting for his signal.

"Con never showed up." Steve spoke unceremoniously as he climbed into the front seat of the car.

"Holy cow! You scared the heck out of me, Steve!" Matt hadn't even known anyone was around when the door was jerked open and the man had dropped into the seat.

Steve glared at Matt and then snickered. "Good thing I wasn't a cop, then, huh? And didn't the boss tell you to stay alert?"

Matt mumbled something about how he was alert. Then he questioned Steve, "So what's going on? What should we do?"

"We should leave. You need to drop me back at my hotel and then you need to go home," Steve told him. "And before you go home, dump this car someplace."

"What if the boss still wants to use it?" Simpson questioned his friend.

"Remember where you left it. If it's still there, fine. If not, I can get us another one." Steve looked out the window thoughtfully for a moment. "Either way, we can't leave it parked in front of your place, now, can we?"

Matt pulled out onto the street and turned left to head toward the hotel the boss had Steve staying in. It wasn't nearly as nice as where Conrad Meyer was staying. He wondered why Steve put up with that.

"We've got a tail." Steve spoke calmly. "Just don't do anything illegal and keep driving," he told Matt.

Flashing red and blue lights pulled in front of them and blocked the street. Red and blue lights lit up the car behind them as well. Steve shrugged. "Okay, Matt, here's how this plays out."

Matt was not happy Steve expected him to take the fall for the stolen car. Since he had never been in trouble before, he would most likely get off on just probation. Steve, on the other hand, had a record. He would go away for a long time. Matt stopped the car, put it in park, and put both hands on the steering wheel. Steve had both hands on the dash in front of him.

By morning Steve was back at his hotel room. Matt was in a holding cell waiting for a judge to arrive and make a ruling. He really hoped Steve was right about that probation thing. Ever since his daddy went to jail, Matt got panic attacks in small places.

Craig Adams drove through Missouri until he had passed Fort Leonard Wood before he found another rest stop and pulled in for a couple hours of sleep. He figured he would get up to the Chicago area in plenty of time to check into a nice hotel, take a hot shower, and find a nice restaurant for his evening meal. Tomorrow he would find his way to Centerville and find Lori.

Once he had taken care of Lori, he needed to decide on his future. He knew he would have to go back to work before too long, but a month off someplace where it wouldn't get too hot this summer would be nice. Maybe he would just go up into Wisconsin.

Steve tried to call Conrad as soon as he got back to his room. When it dawned on him that Meyer could be in jail himself, he gave up. Then he decided to skip town. Pittsburgh held no appeal for him, even though it was his home. He needed to be somewhere else entirely. Remembering he had a cousin out in Washington state, he loaded up his car and checked out of the hotel. By noon he was in Kansas.

Charles Arnold, aka Craig Adams, checked into a hotel in Aurora using his alias. He was glad he had thought to get that paperwork sorted out before leaving Oklahoma. And he knew he needed to be careful. He only had one more set of new IDs with him. Too bad his friend who had forged these new IDs got caught. He couldn't make Charles any new ones while he was sitting in a prison cell.

After a shower and a shave, he walked out onto the street and had a look up and down. Seeing a large, old building off to the east, he started walking in that direction. Maybe it was a bank?

Matt Simpson was out on bail by noon. He headed back to his rooms thinking he would get his car and go find Steve. He wanted to know what had happened to Meyer.

"I'm sorry, sir. Your friend checked out a couple hours ago," the young girl at the desk told Matt.

"Huh?" he questioned.

"He didn't leave any information about where he was going," she added, seeming to think Simpson was expecting more information.

"Okay. Thanks." Muttering "for nothing" under his breath, Matt strode out of the building. As soon as he was in his car, he punched in Steve's number. When the phone went straight to voice mail, Matt hung up. Something was going on. Something bad.

A few minutes later, he found himself on the road to the cemetery. *I need to talk to daddy*, he decided. *Ain't nobody here to tell me I can't now.*

"Steve Leavell is in the wind," Sergeant Mason let Detective Mitchell know. "We weren't able to hold him. Simpson claimed Leavell didn't know he'd stolen the car. And there was nothing there to tie them to any bank robberies." Mason blew out a breath.

"Where's Simpson? He make bail?" Mitchell inquired. He was even more frustrated than his sergeant was. They needed to stop these guys.

"He did make bail. He went back to his rooms and then left about forty-five minutes later." Mason brought the detective up to date. "Right now, he's sittin' by his folks' tombstone out at the cemetery."

"Arnold is definitely in the wind." Mitchell let out a huff. "No one even saw him leave the gallery last night. I've got a man pulling camera footage from all the businesses and traffic lights around there. Hopefully we'll turn something up."

Craig took a seat by the window and stared out and across the street at the old bank building. If he could just pull off one job by himself, and get a big enough haul, he would be set for life. He thought about it all the way through his meal.

Taking a long walk around the neighborhood, around the bank, he made his way slowly back to his hotel. After having a couple drinks in the bar, he took his leave back to his room and watched the baseball game until he finally fell asleep.

"Pastor Stout? Detective Snyder here. I've got a bit of bad news."
The detective began to explain to Marcus what was going on in
Tulsa. "Arnold was seen going into the art gallery across from the
bank we thought he would hit next. No one saw him leave. That
was Thursday night, night before last."

Taking a deep breath and letting it out in a huff, he added,
"No one has seen him since, and he checked out of his hotel later
that evening. We thought you and the missus should know what's
going on."

"You think he's here? In Centerville?" Marcus asked. A note of
concern tinged his question.

"It's a possibility," Snyder told him. "We honestly have no clue,"
he confessed apologetically.

Marcus stood from his seat behind the desk in his church
office. He paced as he questioned the detective and listened to his
less-than-informative answers. "What about the other two men who
worked for him? What are they up to?" he wanted to know.

Sighing deeply, Snyder responded honestly. "Steve Leavell
has vanished too. We are pretty sure he is not with Arnold. Matt
Simpson is out on bail for being caught behind the wheel of a stolen
car. Leavell was with him, but Simpson swore the man didn't know
he had stolen the car." Blowing out a breath, he added, "Leavell
has a pretty long rap sheet. And he's been known to steal a car or
two, but . . ."

"But Simpson has no record and took the fall for him," Marcus
finished the Detective's sentence for him.

"We'll keep you posted, Pastor. You and Mrs. Stout just be
careful and be safe. Stay aware of your surroundings. I'm beefing
up patrol in your neighborhood just as a precaution," Snyder added
before hanging up to take another call.

Matt Simpson's trip to the cemetery had netted him nothing but
the sure knowledge that he was being followed. He drove back to
town, bought enough groceries and beer to last him several days,
and went back to hole up in his rooms and wait for the heat to die
down, and word from Steve or the boss.

He still had no idea what was going on, but he knew it was bad. He hadn't prayed since his daddy went to jail. Now he prayed that he wouldn't end up in jail himself.

The trip to Washington state was long and dull. The radio in his car didn't work, so Steve drove with the windows down, hoping the fresh air would keep him alert. He could not afford to have an accident. He needed to make it to Bellevue, Washington, with law enforcement none the wiser.

While driving through Kansas, he thought to remove the battery from his phone. He wanted to ditch it, but not being able to hear from Meyer was too great a risk. He settled for buying another pay-as-you-go phone to use. He would only put the battery back in his old phone once a day to see if he had missed any texts or calls.

"Snyder," the Detective answered the call on his office phone.

"It's Mitchell. I wanted to give you an update, such as it is." Stewart Mitchell continued, "Simpson has been holed up in his rooms since he left the cemetery yesterday. My blue saw him loading up on groceries and beer before he headed back home. Seems he's decided to lay low for a while."

"What about Leavell and Arnold? Any news on them?" Snyder was concerned about his pastor and his lovely wife's safety.

"We got a ping on Leavell's cell phone just over the state line in Kansas. And Arnold's phone hasn't pinged for us at all," Mitchell confessed, shaking his head in frustration. "We did find out he rented a car at the airport. The onboard GPS tracked him to a rest stop just across the Missouri state line. We've checked the rest stop; the car isn't there. Apparently he disabled the GPS." Scowling, Mitchell almost felt like he needed to apologize to Snyder. He didn't. Both men knew how their jobs worked.

"When was that?" Snyder wanted to know.

"Shortly after 1:00 AM on Friday morning," Mitchell let him know. Then he added, "He used a new ID to rent the car. Called himself Craig Adams."

"They recognized his photo at the airport rental?" Snyder asked. The question was rhetorical.

"Yeah, it was him. Wandered in with some other folks from a flight that had just landed."

"Okay. Thanks for the info. Keep me posted." Snyder knew Mitchell and his team were doing their best. He chose not to give the man any more grief than he sensed he was already dealing with. He knew Mitchell had a strong friendship with both Pastor Marcus and Lori. He knew the man would move Heaven and earth to keep them safe, as would he.

With that in mind, the man called his pastor for the second time on this Saturday morning and filled him in on what Mitchell had just told him.

Sunday morning dawned bright and beautiful. The sunshine and lack of breeze guaranteed the day would be a real scorcher. Marcus put the finishing touches on his sermon before joining Lori in the kitchen for breakfast.

"Thank you, Father, for this beautiful day and for the abundant meal you have provided for us. Lord, we ask that you keep us safe and defeat our enemies. Amen," he prayed over their bacon and scrambled eggs.

"Amen," Lori intoned, then struck up a conversation about what was weighing on her mind. "Honey, you never did tell me about your conversation with Detective Snyder yesterday," she chided him. "Don't you think I need to know? Are we in danger?" she asked.

"Snyder doesn't know if we're in danger or not," Marcus told her. He toyed with his napkin as he gathered his thoughts. This was not a conversation he wanted to have. But Lori was right; she needed to know what was going on. His hesitation was foolish at best, deadly at worst.

"Simpson is still in Tulsa, but Leavell and Arnold are both in the wind. The last they knew of Arnold's whereabouts was a ping on the GPS in a car he rented. He was just across the state line in Missouri."

"So he's on his way here." It wasn't a question.

"If the ping meant he was coming here, then he would already be here. That was early Friday morning." Marcus shook his head as he reached out to grasp his wife's hand. "Lori, I'm sorry. I should have told you all this yesterday."

Lori clung to her husband's hand and tried to smile as a tear dared to slide down her cheek. Swiping at it, she responded, "It's okay, Marcus. I get that talking about it makes it real—too real." She squeezed his hand. "Did Detective Snyder say anything about what we should do?" she asked.

Heaving a breath, Marcus looked at his wife, her beautiful green eyes, the golden locks that fell past her shoulders—shoulders that to Marcus were once again weighed down with the cares of a world she had long ago left behind. "He said they were beefing up patrols around our neighborhood and we should be careful and keep our eyes open." He decided to add, "Keep our doors locked, even at the church. Don't go outside, not even with the trash, without making sure the other of us is aware. And I just added those cautions, but I think they're worthy ideas."

Lori nodded her agreement. "Okay. We both need to leave for church at the same time this morning. Safety in numbers and all that." Standing up, she began clearing the table. Marcus retreated to his home office to grab his sermon notes and Bible. They would cross the lawn together.

CHAPTER NINETEEN

---------†---------

Charles Arnold bought an Illinois road map at a local truck stop. Not having a GPS was such a hassle, but he didn't dare turn it back on. He wasn't even sure he knew how.

There was very little traffic as he headed west out of Aurora on a bright and warm Sunday morning. Knowing Marcus was a preacher, he figured he could find him by looking for his car in the parking lots of the churches in town. The older-model blue Chevy would be easy to spot. As he drove up and down the streets of Centerville, he counted seven churches. He saw no old blue Chevy's. He didn't see Michah's older black Pontiac either.

Furious, he drove around town and up and down the streets till after 2:00 that afternoon. Had Matt been wrong about where the couple had gone? It wouldn't be the first time he'd made a mistake.

"Snyder." The Detective answered the phone in his office, distraction and impatience in his voice.

"Mitchell here." Detective Stewart Mitchell was anything but distracted this morning. "We know how Arnold got away."

Mitchell briefed Snyder on the information he had gotten first thing that morning. "One of the employees at the art gallery called this morning to report the theft of a blond wig from her unlocked locker. It was taken sometime between 2:00 Thursday afternoon and 6:00 this morning. We have camera footage of someone in a maintenance jumpsuit leaving by the back door and putting a trash bag in the dumpster." Pausing for a breath, he finished, "They had long, blond hair."

Snyder sat up and pulled his pen and pad closer. "Any idea which way he went after he dumped the trash bag?"

"The blues are canvassing the area. There is no other camera footage, but we're checking the dumpsters up and down the alley. The one behind the gallery held only trash. Two doors down, there was a maintenance jumpsuit. We're processing it."

"Hopefully you'll find the wig too. That could have a stray hair or two for a positive DNA match." Snyder's excitement had grown. Maybe, just maybe, they were finally getting somewhere.

"Actually, we have the wig," Mitchell told him, a note of satisfaction ringing in his voice. "We're processing it too."

Reality sunk in. Snyder had to add, "We still don't know where he went."

Sighing deeply, Mitchell admitted, "No, we don't."

"Okay then; let's assume he headed for Centerville," Snyder suggested. "There are no hotels in town and just one small bed and breakfast. I'll check it out, but I doubt he'd be there."

"No, probably not." Mitchell chimed in on the what-if scenario. "He would want to be someplace bigger, someplace it would be easier to blend in and disappear. Maybe even someplace with a bank nearby."

"I'll talk to a couple friends at the department over in Aurora," Snyder responded thoughtfully. "There is an older bank downtown, and it does have a hotel just down the block."

"If there's a nice restaurant nearby, I'd say that would be the spot," Mitchell suggested.

"Marcus, you haven't forgotten we are taking Miss Kay to the hospital tomorrow, have you?" Katherine Blanchett was a much-loved older member of Faith Unfolding Chapel. Two years ago she had had a stroke and lost the use of her legs. Tomorrow she was going into the hospital in Aurora for a series of tests to see if there was anything her doctors could do to restore their use.

"No. No, I haven't. We are going. I've already let Detective Snyder know what's going on. He says he can beef up security around the hospital for one day." Marcus was nervous about leaving the safe shelter of their home, but he would not allow evil to keep him from his church family. Miss Kay would need his and Lori's presence tomorrow.

"Detective Snyder." The man picked up on the first ring.

Marcus rebriefed him on the plans for the day. "Miss Kay will be at the hospital in Aurora for tests tomorrow. Lori and I intend to take her and be there with her all day."

Snyder smiled to himself before he responded, a serious tone in his voice. "It's good of you to be there for her, Pastor. I have passed the info on to my Aurora contacts. If anything changes, if you need to go back there again another day, be sure to let me know." Hanging up the phone, he smiled again. He prayerfully hoped there would be no danger tomorrow — or any other day.

Pastor Marcus and Lori took their roles as shepherds of the flock of Faith Unfolding Chapel seriously. Snyder respected them for that. He admired their tenacity.

The Stouts sat quietly in the waiting room outside the surgical unit Miss Kay had been wheeled into. Both reflected on their lives as they were unfolding here in their new home.

"It would be wonderful if the doctors could help her walk again." Lori finally spoke her thoughts.

"Yes, it would," Marcus agreed. "She seems to be content with her life as it is, though." He had to add, "It doesn't seem to have slowed her down very much."

"From what I hear, it hasn't slowed her down at all." Lori smiled as she spoke. It hadn't taken long for them to understand what an integral part of Faith Unfolding Chapel Miss Kay was. She loved everyone, and everyone loved her.

"Pastor? Mrs. Lori? What are you doing here?" A somewhat familiar male voice spoke from near the bank of elevators. David Harris was unsuccessful at hiding his surprise at seeing his pastor and his pastor's wife sitting in the waiting room of the surgical unit.

Marcus stood up and stuck out his hand as he walked toward the obviously surprised older man. Shaking hands with him, he explained, "Miss Kay is here for some tests today, so here we are too." He spoke as if no one should expect him to be elsewhere.

"Oh! That's right. I remember now." An obviously flustered response came from David.

"What brings you here, David?" Concern and curiosity tinged Lori's voice.

Heaving a heavy sigh, David motioned to the nearby sofa and took a seat himself. "Connie, my wife, has been having some unusual health issues, so we decided it was time to check it out."

His face clouded and he struggled to speak. "We found out she has colon cancer. They're doing surgery now to see how much of it they can get."

Marcus glanced at his wife as he put an arm across the crying man's shoulders. "We will pray with you," he said as he bowed his head and worked to find the words of comfort he needed to say. "Father, give them peace and comfort. Hold them close and provide them the gentle touch of healing only You can provide," the prayer began.

The threesome sat in comfortable silence for a few moments, soaking up the peace that had encompassed them.

"David, why have we not heard about this before?" Lori gently asked.

Heaving a sigh, David scrubbed a hand down his face and worked to find the words to explain. "Our son, Nick, is deployed in Afghanistan right now. He doesn't know anything about any of this. Yet. We haven't told anyone because everyone sends him cards and letters and care packages, and we didn't want him hearing it from someone else."

Shaking his head, he continued, "We're going to have to tell him now. Soon. And we probably should have told him sooner, but . . . ." He trailed off, unable to find the words.

"We will keep this to ourselves," Lori assured him. "But you're right, you need to tell him now."

"Does your daughter, Jenny, know?" Lori thought to ask the man.

"Yes. Yes, she knows." Seeming to hesitate, David continued, "She should be here any minute now. Her husband needed her to take care of something for him first. There's not much she could do here anyhow . . . ." He trailed off again.

Lori glanced over at her husband. Marcus's barely visible nod sent a small shiver down Lori's spine. They had heard the whispers. Everyone at Faith Unfolding Chapel cared about each other, and innocent, unintentional gossip worked its way around through the prayer chains that were frequently formed.

Jenny was married to an abusive man. Lori wondered if she would make it to the hospital at all today.

Thankfully, Jenny did show up. She hugged her father close and cried into his chest for several minutes before she even seemed to notice Lori and Marcus. Wiping her eyes, she struggled to compose herself. Her hand shook as she reached out to briefly clasp Lori's as they introduced themselves. "So good to finally meet you, Jenny," Lori said. "Your dad talks about you often. We can tell you're very close."

Jenny nodded and mumbled a quiet "Nice to meet you too."

The doctor came out to let Lori and Marcus know that Miss Kay had been taken to recovery. "She is still sedated," he explained. "It will be at least half an hour before she starts coming out of it. Everything went according to plan during surgery. It will be about ten days before the results come back," he let them know.

Marcus nodded his understanding and, turning to his wife, suggested, "Let's go grab a bite of lunch and then head to recovery."

Lori nodded and invited David and Jenny to join them. Jenny shook her head and David politely declined. "Thank you, but I think we'll sit tight for now."

The doctor went back down the hall toward the surgical unit, and Lori and Marcus took the elevator down to the cafeteria.

When they came back up forty minutes later, David and Jenny were gone. "Remind me to call David in the morning and find out how things went today," Marcus requested of Lori. They had both quickly found that it was easier to keep track of everything if they worked together as a team.

Lori had a small calendar she kept in her purse and made a note to call David on the next day's page. "I guess this is a really old-fashioned way to do this," She commented. "But after the day I forgot to charge my phone and you were late for that meeting, it just seems smarter."

"I think it's way more convenient," Marcus told her. "I can pull your calendar out and check the date's activities twice as fast as I can pull up the calendar page on your phone."

Their quiet conversation continued until a nurse summoned them to Miss Kay's recovery room. When the doctor came in a short time later, he informed them that Miss Kay would be spending the night, just as a precautionary measure. "She should be ready to scoot out of here in time for lunch tomorrow," he smilingly let them know.

Miss Kay grumbled and Lori reminded her of their early morning conversation. "You told me you didn't want anyone having to go home with you and stay till you recovered. It doesn't look like that's going to need to happen."

"This is not what I meant to happen either." The woman pouted good-naturedly. "Will I never learn to be more careful what I ask for? God always gives me what I need, not what I want," she finished with a grin.

Lori and Pastor Marcus stayed until Miss Kay was settled comfortably in her room. Promising to be back before noon the next day, they headed through the door.

"Pastor?" Miss Kay called out to them.

Marcus stuck his head back through the door. "Yes, ma'am?" he questioned.

"Please, just go ahead and take my car home with you. It will save you a lot of time, and you'll need it tomorrow too," she suggested. "It's not hard to drive at all. The pedals still work, so you can use them instead of the hand controls," she added with a wink.

He nodded his understanding and said, "Okay. Thank you. We will do that." He pulled the door shut and he and Lori headed out into the late afternoon sunshine.

"Now I really wish I hadn't let Miss Kay do the driving this morning," Marcus grumbled good–naturedly as he struggled to get comfortable in the driver's seat of a car owned by a woman a full eight inches shorter than him. Then he had to figure out how to drive without bumping into her special handicap-friendly controls.

After driving around for the better part of the day Monday, Arnold found the old blue Chevy he knew belonged to Mark Stout, the preacher. It was parked in the lot at some old folks' apartments. It was still there when Charles left at 9:00 that evening. He was hungry and bored, and nature was calling. He had sat there five hours and nothing had happened. He decided that just knowing he was in the right town was good enough for today.

Just to double check, he drove back by after relieving himself and getting a meal. The car was still there. *Probably died and they can't afford a tow truck,* he thought to himself.

On Tuesday morning he cruised into Centerville and swung by the senior living facility. The car was still there. He left town and spent the rest of the day working on a plan to eliminate Lori and rob one last bank before he retired. "I like the sound of that." he said to himself and smiled. "Retired. And rich."

"Hey, Mitchell," Detective Snyder answered his cell phone. "Everything all right?" he wanted to know.

"All is well here," Detective Mitchell responded. "Just needing an update from you," he added.

"Pastor and Lori spent the day in Aurora yesterday. One of our church family had some tests run and they took her and stayed with her all day." Snyder ran through the brief update. "They are back there today to pick her up and take her home."

"No sign of Arnold?" Mitchell questioned.

"He is checked into a hotel near downtown Aurora, and he's using the alias Craig Adams. The blues there are keeping an eye on him," Snyder told him. "He is trying to find the Stouts. We're certain of that. He's driven up and down the streets of Centerville at least a dozen times." The man actually chuckled. "And he's casing the bank down there near his hotel," he added, sobering quickly.

"Marcus and Lori know about this, yes?" Mitchell had sat straight up in his chair, as if Snyder could see through the cell phone connection how seriously he was taking this bit of news.

"Yes. They know." Detective Snyder filled him in. "I spoke with Pastor Marcus late yesterday afternoon and let him know what's going on." He went on to explain, "My undercover guys had a bit of a scare at first. They knew Pastor's car would be parked at the Senior Living Facility and were discreetly keeping an eye on it when a rental car with Oklahoma plates pulled into the lot. They made sure the driver didn't see them. They also discovered the man matches Arnold's description. It's rented to Craig Adams."

Snyder also thought to add, "When we traced it back to the rental company to find out who it was rented to, they confirmed that the GPS had been disabled just across the Missouri state line."

"That's him!" Mitchell was ready to do a happy dance in his chair. "Watch him," he requested. "And make sure your men know how good he is at giving us the slip."

"Roger that," Snyder responded and then ended the call. The Stouts were due to drop Miss Kay off at her house around 1:00, and he wanted to be there when they arrived.

When his office phone rang five minutes later, he picked up on the first ring. "Snyder," he stated simply.

"We're leaving the hospital now," Marcus told him.

"Okay." Snyder then began to fill the young pastor in. "Arnold found your car at Miss Kay's," he warned him. "We've had eyes on your car since you parked it yesterday. There shouldn't be a problem."

"So we're going to be good to go?" Marcus wanted to know.

"No." Snyder shook his head as he spoke. "We aren't going to assume anything. You are to call a tow truck as soon as you arrive. Do not go anywhere near the car. Instead of a tow truck, you will actually be calling an undercover who will come out undercover as a tow truck driver."

Snyder had the plan well laid-out. "He has skills with bombs, and he has a bomb-sniffing canine that will accompany him. If there is no bomb detected, your car will be towed and you and your wife will ride with him to the auto repair shop. Then you can have your car back. If we find a bomb or any evidence of tampering, that will change everything. Whatever happens, you will need to do exactly as your tow truck driver tells you to do." Snyder paused to let that soak in a bit. Then, "Understood?" he needed to know.

"Yes, sir." Marcus understood. He was frightened by the seriousness of the situation. And he understood *that* completely.

After making sure Pastor Stout had the number he would need to call, Snyder rang off and headed out the door to his black sedan. It was a short drive to the facility, but he wasn't going there. He would shoot past it, as were several other undercovers and blues.

They would trickle back on foot or they would be parked scattered out around the neighborhood.

One old, rusty Toyota Camry sat in the lot. It had been driven in shortly after Arnold had been spotted near the lot. The plainclothes female who had driven it had spent the night in a vacant second-floor apartment with eyes on Charles and the Stouts' old blue car.

A new plainclothes officer had shown up at seven this morning to take her place while she napped on an air mattress in the bedroom. Both would be in position and ready for a takedown by one this afternoon. Snyder had high hopes they would actually pull it off this time.

Detective Snyder parked his car a block down in the back lot of an insurance office. Invisible from the street, he walked quickly down an alley that hadn't seen a load of gravel in a decade. Ruts of dried mud attested to the continuing use of the weed-bordered lane. The man pulled up short behind a smelly dumpster and clicked his shoulder mic. "Everyone better be in position. Miss Kay's Cadillac is coming down the street."

Marcus pulled into the Senior Living Facility lot and pulled right up to the front door. An officer had given him, Lori, and even Miss Kay bulletproof vests before they left the hospital. The weight of it pulled at Marcus and slowed him down as he pushed himself out of the driver's seat and headed to the back of the car to retrieve the older woman's wheelchair. Lori and Miss Kay both stayed in the car.

He pushed the chair up to the woman's car door and then paused, pulling the paper and his phone from his pocket. He glanced over at his old blue Chevy and then dialed the number Detective Snyder had given him.

"I'm on my way, Pastor Stout," the strange voice answered the phone. "You're all clear to get the ladies inside, and I suggest you do it quickly. I will call you when it's time for you to join me in the parking lot." Marcus barely had time to respond in acknowledgment before the man hung up.

He quickly helped Miss Kay into the chair and then Lori led the way and Marcus pushed the chair as they hurried inside. All three breathed a sigh of relief when the apartment door closed behind them and Marcus turned the deadbolt and locked it.

"Well, that was quite the adventure," Miss Kay chuckled. "I was sort of hoping for a little more excitement," she added, and then chuckled at herself. "No, not really."

Then Miss Kay requested, "Lori, will you put the teakettle on for me, please? I would very much enjoy a cup of chamomile tea." She kept her hands clasped together in her lap, but Lori could tell they were shaking.

"Of course." Lori was happy to comply. "Can I do anything else for you?" she wanted to know.

Miss Kay had wheeled over to her table and picked up her Bible. She held it lovingly in her hands. "No, dear. A cup of tea is all that I'm missing right now."

Lori had barely set the cup of steeping tea on the table when Marcus's phone rang. A brief conversation later, and he said, "Honey, they're ready to take us to the auto shop."

A quick hug and a nod of understanding from Miss Kay and the two left the apartment and headed for the building's parking lot exit.

"Stay close to me." Marcus didn't need to tell Lori as she had already snuggled herself up under his protective arm. "Be ready to climb in the truck as soon as I get the door open," he added.

The tow driver saw them coming and opened the passenger door for them. He stood between Marcus and possible danger as Marcus helped Lori in and then climbed in beside her.

It was more than an hour later before they were finally on their way back to Centerville.

"Why did we have to stay at the shop so long?" Lori wanted to know.

Marcus merged into the traffic on the interstate before he responded. "They were making sure we hadn't been tailed, I think. And I know they gave the car a more thorough going-over," he added.

"You mean there could have still been a bomb in it when we hauled it across town?" Lori looked at her husband in disbelief.

"No, sweetheart, no. They were looking for trackers and bugs at the shop." If the situation hadn't been so gravely serious, Marcus would have laughed out loud. It was a breath of fresh air to see Lori still had some innocence about her, after all she had been through.

She snorted and then chuckled. When it became a full-on laugh, Marcus laughed too. The tension eased. The peace of God returned and enveloped them.

Once their car was parked safely in their garage, they both felt as though they could move forward with some sense of normalcy.

"I need to work on my sermon," Marcus told her and continued down the hall to his study.

"I'll start supper," Lori stated. "Pork chops okay?"

"You know they're my favorite!" Marcus called out as he pushed the study door closed. Then, thinking better of it, he left it open. He could hear his wife humming in the kitchen as the pots and pans rattled and the refrigerator door opened and closed.

The sounds of normalcy, he thought to himself, deciding he could live with those sounds and actually wanted to hear them — enjoyed hearing them.

When Marcus's cell phone rang a few minutes later, he checked the caller ID and saw it was Detective Snyder. "Yes, sir?" he answered with a note of questioning in his voice.

"Hello, Pastor," the detective responded calmly.

The reassuring tone calmed Marcus considerably. "Anything going on?" Marcus asked hesitantly. No news always seemed to be the best news, and a phone call from Detective Snyder rarely brought good news.

"Believe it or not, I have some good news." Marcus heard the smile in the man's voice. Snyder continued, "Arnold was just spotted in a restaurant across the street from a bank in downtown Aurora. And we think he may have been in that area all day." Then, hesitantly, the man added, "Hopefully he's been there all day."

Breathing a sigh of relief, Marcus responded in the only way he knew how. "Praise the Lord!" There was excitement in his voice. "So you don't think he followed us or knows where we live?"

"That is our belief at this point," the Detective answered cautiously. "We are still keeping the patrols beefed up in your neighborhood, and I am asking a lot of questions of the blues assigned to this case in Aurora. I know the man is slippery, but I need to know how they failed to see where he went when he left his hotel this morning." Shaking his head in disbelief, he voiced his thoughts: "That should have been a simple enough thing to do."

Realizing what he had just done, showing a lack of trust in fellow law enforcement, he quickly added, "There's a lot more going on in Aurora on any given day than there is here in Centerville. I'm sure there is a reasonable explanation."

Marcus decided to leave all that alone for now and chose instead to ask, "Can Lori and I go grocery shopping today? We haven't been for several days now, and she told me earlier that I needed to find out how soon we could go."

"How soon will you be able to go?" Snyder asked.

"Lori's cooking supper right now, so not for an hour or so," Marcus responded.

"Okay. We can work with that," Snyder told him, then asked, "Where do you do your shopping?"

"There's a big store on the other side of town, near the interstate. We always go there."

Pastor Marcus and the detective worked out the details and rang off. When Marcus looked up, Lori was standing in the doorway. "That sounded like a lot of good news," she stated. "While our supper cooks, I'll get the grocery list ready. You can tell me about the conversation while we eat." She gave him the eye that told him she had heard enough that she would know if he left anything out.

Honestly, he thought to himself, *Lori reads me even better than Michah!* Shaking his head, he sat at his desk and went back to his notes. This sermon would be a good one.

CHAPTER TWENTY

———†———

"We're ready whenever you are." Detective Snyder had called Marcus back an hour later.

Marcus glanced at Lori. They were finishing their meal. She rose to start putting things away. "We can be out the door in five minutes," he told the man.

"Leave the dishes. I will help with them later," Marcus suggested. "Let's just go."

Nodding her agreement, Lori reached for her purse and grabbed the list from the counter. "Lord keep us safe," she spoke a simple prayer.

"Amen," Marcus intoned as he closed and locked the door.

Once in the car, he pushed the button to raise the garage door and backed down the driveway.

The only traffic on the street was a police car that passed as they exited the garage and, after turning around in the church parking lot, followed them down the street.

"Why did he turn off?" Lori wanted to know when she saw the patrol car make a left as they continued straight through the center of town.

Marcus nodded toward the windshield. "That black sedan that pulled in front of us is Detective Snyder," he explained.

They rode in silence, behind the black sedan, the rest of the way to the super center.

The lot was packed with cars. Marcus tried, and failed, to find a spot near the doors. "Park close to the detective," Lori suggested and jerked a thumb in the direction she had seen Snyder head.

Marcus pulled in two cars before him, nearer the store. "Let's just get this over with," he requested as he took Lori's hand and they headed for the doors.

"Stouts are heading in," Detective Snyder said into his radio. "Keep your eyes wide open and on a 360. Arnold needs to be caught." The officers hearing the message also heard the impatience and anger in their supervisor's tone. Snyder was done with Charles Arnold's games.

"Do you remember the first time we shopped together?" Lori asked her husband, trying to lighten the mood.

Marcus looked askance at his wife, then a large smile enveloped his face and brought out the dimples that Lori loved so much. "The day I bought the Charlie Brown tree for you."

Lori nodded and flashed a huge grin at Marcus. "I thought I was falling for you already then. But when you showed up the next day with that tree, I knew I was a goner," she told him.

"I was head over heels by then too," he told her and pulled her in for a quick kiss. "Michah was the one who actually explained to me why I couldn't stop thinking about you . . . why I cared so much about what was happening to you."

After a few moments, Lori spoke into the thoughtful silence. "I miss Michah too, sweetheart."

Changing the subject abruptly, Marcus wanted to know, "Can we get ice cream?"

Lori giggled and nodded as Marcus buried his head in the freezer and came out with a quart of his favorite: Moose Tracks.

They made it through the checkout and back to the car in a comfortably uneventful silence. Heaving a sigh, Marcus started the car and headed back out to the street that would take them home.

Charles Arnold knew he had been made. He pulled into the car rental business and explained to them that the GPS wasn't working and he was tired of getting lost. Less than an hour later, he was back on the street again. He had been given an SUV upgrade.

After a quick bite of supper, he drove over to Centerville and once again cruised the streets as casually as he could. He hated small towns. There was no anonymity there, no place to hide.

The Stouts' car was not at the retirement facility. And he didn't see it at either of the three auto shops in town. Of course, it could be behind one of their big garage doors.

He drove out toward the interstate and pulled into a truck stop. After relieving himself, he bought a multi pack of gum and a large coffee and headed back into town. The coffee was so nasty tasting that he pulled over and dumped it on the side of the road.

Signaling to get back into the driving lane, he looked in his rear view mirror and spotted the old blue Chevy as it turned onto a cross street nearly two blocks back. He thought he remembered a church on that street. He cautiously drove on down the street and further away from where he had seen the car turn off. Not seeing any undercover vehicles, he made a left and drove down as far as that street would take him. It was only seven blocks long. Another left and then another onto the next street over and parallel to the street he had seen the blue car turn onto. Then he saw the under-cover cars. And he thought, a small pickup truck might be an under-cover as well. No one paid any attention to him, and he was glad he had switched vehicles.

"Safe at home," Lori sighed. "As soon as the groceries are put away and the dishes are done, we can have some of that ice cream." She could see the wheels turning in her husband's head. "You put the groceries away." She smiled knowingly at him. "I'll wash the dishes."

Marcus hated doing dishes. He ducked his head and hid a grin as he began emptying the bags and stowing the food and sundries away. "Yes, dear," he said as he chuckled.

Lori finished the dishes as Marcus began retrieving bowls and spoons to fix their ice cream. "I'm going to take out the trash," Lori said, the full bag in her hand as she headed out the back door.

Her husband groaned. He should have thought to do that. He followed her to the door. "Let me," he insisted.

She gladly relinquished the task to him and stood near the door to watch and wait. Darkness had fallen and clouds hid what few stars the nearby city lights didn't mask. Crickets chirping and the soft whoosh of traffic from the street were the only sounds cutting through the stillness of the evening.

The lid rattled on the trash can as Marcus closed it firmly against the stray creatures that he had discovered loved to forage in unsecured garbage cans. "It is a beautiful night," he stated as he walked back through the door. Lori locked it behind him and they retrieved their dishes of ice cream and snuggled up together on the sofa to watch a movie. It was a peaceful ending to a long and frightening day. Lori thanked God for their safety and wondered, and prayed, about tomorrow.

Charles had parked discreetly on the street at the edge of the side yard of what appeared to be an apartment house. It was an older house that had four mailboxes lined up on the wall of the closed-in front porch.

He scooted down low in his seat and kept an eye on the back door of the house, whose yard butted up to the backyard of the apartment house. There was a light on in what he assumed was the kitchen. He was pretty sure Lori was in there. It was next door to the church, and he had taken note of a privacy fence separating the house on the other side of the church from the church property. This house had an attached garage. That would explain why he had never seen the cars.

It was barely ten minutes till the back door opened and a woman silhouetted it. Then she stepped back and a man came out with a trash bag in his hand. Charles snickered as Lori stood, outlined— as beautiful as he remembered—in the backlit doorway. He had found her.

He waited until the two had gone back inside and shut off the light to leave. Then he drove around the block and passed by the front of their house. The only light was the flicker of a television. A lone unmarked car sat on the street two doors down. Shaking his head as he drove on by, Charles Arnold knew now was not the time. "Soon. Very soon," he promised himself.

Arnold could have kicked himself when it dawned on him that the cops probably had eyes on his hotel, and he hadn't checked out and left it before he upgraded his rental car. "Never mind," he told himself as he drove on past it and parked in the lot of a different one on down the street. He would walk down the street tonight. And tomorrow he would figure out what to do to fix his mistake.

"Detective Mitchell here." The man's phone was already ringing when he walked into his office the next morning. And he hadn't had his coffee yet.

The caller introduced himself as an employee of the Airport Car Rental Agency. "We got a phone call late yesterday afternoon from a sister agency in Aurora, Illinois," the man explained. Mitchell listened and started taking notes. The employee went on to tell the detective that a man who had rented a car at his agency in Tulsa had gone into the agency in Aurora complaining that the GPS didn't work, and that agency had swapped him out and upgraded him to an SUV rental. "When the guys in the repair shop got into it and had a closer look, they discovered that the GPS had been purposely disabled," he continued. "That's when they called us."

"You're telling me the man we have a warrant out for is driving an SUV now?" Mitchell needed to know.

"Yes, sir," the man responded, adding, "He's driving a new white Chevy Equinox."

Mitchell was already calling Snyder on his cell phone before he disconnected the call from the rental agency.

Snyder answered on the first ring and heard Mitchell talking to someone else. Wondering briefly if he had been pocket-dialed, he stayed on the line. "Snyder here. Mitchell? Are you there?"

"Yeah, I'm here. Thanks for hanging on," he started, and then continued, "Arnold switched vehicles." He told Detective Snyder what he had just learned from the Tulsa rental agency.

"I'll send someone over to the Aurora agency to go through that car," he promised Mitchell. "Let me get this update out there," he added, and quickly rang off.

His first call was to the Stouts. Lori answered her husband's phone. "Hello. This is Lori Stout."

"Mrs. Stout, Detective Snyder here." She heard the concern in his voice as the man rapidly explained to her what was going on. "You and Pastor need to lay low today and give us a chance to regroup and get eyes on the man again."

"Okay," she said nervously. "Marcus was only planning to be over at the church working on his sermon, but I think he can do that from home." Her knees wobbled so badly she sat down on the kitchen chair. One hand clutched the phone while the other white-knuckled the edge of the table.

"Where is your husband now?" Snyder wanted to know.

Unwilling to lie, Lori confessed, "He's at the church. He forgot his phone this morning."

"Do not leave the house," Snyder ordered. "I'll send the blue on duty out front to the church to let him know, and he can walk him back to the house."

Lori agreed to the plan and Detective Snyder hung up and immediately called his man out front. The officer answered on the first ring. "Yes, sir?"

Explaining quickly what was happening, Snyder got assurances from his blue that it was quiet on the street and he hadn't seen any white SUVs. "I'll go to the church right now and walk the preacher back home," the man assured him.

Snyder hung up and started making other necessary calls.

Charles Arnold had not slept very well the night before. Today was going to be a very long day. By 6:00 he had his bags packed and was in his car on the way to Centerville. He pulled into the super market's parking lot and, parking near the entrance, went inside and bought a few packs of gum, a couple doughnuts, and a large cup of coffee.

Back in his SUV, he decided this coffee was much better than the truck stop coffee. The doughnuts were pretty good too. And it was time to put his plan in motion.

Leaving his car where it was, he walked toward the center of the little town. He was glad he had his walking shoes on. Centerville may have been a small town, but it covered a lot of ground. At 7:30 on a Wednesday morning, the streets were empty, save for the old man's club that had gathered at the little greasy spoon at the end of Main Street.

Charles took to the alleys as he neared the side of town Lori lived on. Most had sheds, garages, fences, or hedges blocking the view of the alley from their kitchen windows.

Hearing, and then seeing, a garage door going up, he pushed himself back into some overgrown hedges two backyards away.

When the car headed down the alley, away from him, Charles heaved a sigh of relief.

Getting his bearings, he continued down the alley until he spotted the back end of the church parking lot. The house next to where the Stouts lived had a tall privacy fence that ran the length of the adjoining backyards. Recalling a real estate company sign in the front yard of this house, Arnold hoped that meant the house was vacant. He walked cautiously to the front end of the fence. *So the little pickup is a cop*, he thought to himself when he saw the same pickup from the night before parked on this street near the far side of the church parking lot.

Pressing himself flat against the fence, he stood quietly thinking about his plan, running through what he intended to do next. Lori would not escape this time.

He was watching when the undercover cop got out of his truck and walked across the church parking lot and up to its big double doors. Now was his chance. Quietly and quickly he slipped around the end of the fence. Bending over low, he worked his way toward the back of the parsonage. Staying below window level and close to the house, he hoped no one inside would be able to see him.

Lori looked out the front window and saw the plainclothes officer get out of his little pickup and walk up to the front doors of the church. She moved to the back door, knowing Marcus would come across the backyard and in the kitchen door. The back door of the church opened and Marcus walked out, his Bible in his hand. *Where's the officer?* she wondered.

Without thinking, she walked out the back door and turned toward the church. "Marcus!" she called out to him. He looked up at her, and then his eyes focused on something behind her.

Charles peeked around the back corner of the parsonage and saw her walk out the back door. "Perfect!" he said to himself and took his stance, revolver held out in front of him like the expert marksman he was not.

"No!" Marcus shouted when he saw Charles Arnold, aka Curtis Maquire, standing at the back of his house with a gun in his hand.

Lori was running toward him, unaware of the danger she was in. Marcus's feet carried him across the distance as though they had wings on them. He grabbed his beautiful wife by the arm and practically slung her behind him as the shot cracked through the late summer air.

Marcus hit the ground hard. Lori was sprawled out beside him. He thought he heard more shots fired, but his world was closing in on him and he couldn't have said for sure. The only thing he was certain of was that his chest was on fire.

"Marcus? Marcus!" Lori screamed at him. "No! Oh, God! Please, no!" She was screaming hysterically. Her beloved husband lay on the ground. He was not moving.

She was vaguely aware of the plainclothes officer from out front coming up beside her and bending over Marcus. "He's got a pulse," he stated as he called it in. Moments later Lori heard sirens coming closer.

"Ma'am, we need to get your husband to the hospital." The officer took her arm and guided her to the ambulance, helping her to climb in and sit on the bench beside Marcus. She took her husband's hand and held on tight, willing him to live.

CHAPTER TWENTY-ONE

———————†———————

"**P**astor Stout? Can you hear me?" Someone was talking to him. He tried to open his eyes, but the light was so bright it hurt. He thought he must be in Heaven. Wanting desperately to see his Jesus, he willed his eyes open.

"He's awake." The man spoke again. Was that what God sounded like?

"Marcus. Sweetheart. Please be okay." He heard Lori talking and tears filled his eyes. She was in Heaven too. He tried to save her life and now could only be grateful her soul was saved. They could be together for eternity.

"What happened, Officer Smith?" Snyder had arrived on the scene moments after Lori and Marcus had been hauled away to the trauma unit.

"Arnold snuck up on me," Officer Jackson—Jax—Smith admitted. His hands still shook, and he clasped them together to try and still them. "I left my truck and walked over to the church to get the preacher and walk him back home. I buzzed the buzzer at the front entrance and was standing there waiting for a response when I heard Mrs. Stout call out to her husband." The officer paused and looked at the man lying dead on the ground.

"I heard the Preacher yell out like he was scared as I was jumping off the side of the steps. The shot went off as I was rounding the corner. The man shot at Mrs. Stout. I shot back." He pulled his gun from its holster and handed it, grip first, to Detective Snyder. "I didn't want to kill him, but I had to keep him from killing Mrs. Stout."

The detective put an arm around the young rookie's shoulders. "You did your job, Officer." He looked the young man in the eye. "I will see to it that you get this back as soon as you're ready for it," he told him as he placed the revolver in an evidence bag.

Marcus sat up in the hospital bed with Lori in the chair beside him. "Honey, you should go home and get some rest," Marcus tried to convince her. She just looked at him with those big green eyes he had fallen into many months ago and shook her head.

"At least go check on Miss Kay," he very nearly begged.

Again his wife just stared at him and shook her head. "Miss Kay is fine," she told him. "I talked to her a couple hours ago. And *I. Am. Not. Leaving!*" Lori informed him.

Sighing deeply, then groaning because it made his chest hurt, Marcus gave up. He felt his eyes drift shut. They popped open again when he heard voices in the room. Lori was talking to a man. The voice seemed familiar.

"Mrs. Stout, I am so glad Pastor is okay," Detective Snyder told her, briefly clasping her hand and smiling as he spoke. "We do need to get statements from both of you," he added, quickly switching back into cop mode. Then he thought to add, "Please."

Lori nodded her understanding and tried to organize her thoughts to tell him what she remembered happening. "You called Marcus's phone and I answered. After you told me Curtis—er, Charles Arnold—had a different car, I walked to the front window and saw your officer get out of his pickup truck and walk over to the front doors of the church. Then I went to the back door to wait for Marcus to come across the yard."

She continued, "I saw him walk out the side door and head across the yard, but the officer wasn't with him," she continued. "It dawned on me that maybe he hadn't heard the buzzer up front. You have to push it really hard and hold it down for it to actually work," she explained. "Then I stepped out into the yard to call out to Marcus and tell him to hurry." Tears formed in the corners of her eyes and began to flow freely down her cheeks.

Swiping at them, she heaved a breath and continued, "Marcus shouted back at me. He sounded so scared. Terrified. And he was running at me. He grabbed my arm," she glanced down at a big bruise on her forearm, "and literally threw me behind him." Swiping at the tears, she continued, "I lost my balance and hit the ground. I heard the gunshot as I was falling."

Managing a brief and watery smile, she looked up at the detective. "At first I thought I had heard the bone in my arm snap from Marcus jerking on it." Sobering, she finished, "When I saw him on the ground and heard another gunshot, I knew he had saved my life. And my arm wasn't broken."

Detective Snyder wrote it all down. Then, setting aside the notepad and pen, he pulled out his cell phone and, opening up the photo gallery, said, "I have to show you this." He scrolled through several pictures and then tapped one and enlarged it to the full screen.

Lori saw a large leather bound Bible. It looked like the one Marcus always carried. "Is that Marcus's?" she asked.

Snyder nodded his head in affirmation and then pointed to the center of the leather cover. "That's the hole the bullet made. That's why your husband, and my pastor, is still alive."

Lori's eyes grew wide as she stared at the huge hole in the middle of Marcus's Bible. "He has always said this book is his shield."

"May I see it too?" Marcus's voice came from the bed behind them. He had heard most of the exchange.

The Detective stepped closer to the bed and held out his phone with the picture of Marcus's Bible and the hole in the center of it easily visible to the man propped against the pillows.

Lori reclaimed her husband's hand and he squeezed it gently. "I'm so sorry I bruised your arm, sweetheart," Marcus apologized. In response, Lori bent over him and kissed him firmly on the lips.

Grinning, she spoke mischievously, "I'll let you slide this time. But it better never happen again!" For good measure, she bent over and kissed him again.

After taking Marcus's statement, Detective Snyder returned to the police station. He had a lot of work to do. Picking up the phone, he called the now-familiar number of Detective Mitchell in Tulsa.

"Charles Arnold is dead," he told him without preamble.

After a beat, Mitchell responded, "What happened? Tell me everything."

Derrick Snyder was happy to comply. Ending the tale with, "I never really believed those old war stories about guys surviving a bullet because of their Bible until I saw it happen today," a note of awe in his voice.

Mitchell responded, "I guess I'm a believer now too. And actually, I was about to call you." He had his own news to share. "We picked up Simpson on a DUI." Detective Mitchell filled Snyder in on his latest report on the Charles Arnold case. "He started spilling the beans on Arnold almost as soon as we booked him. Seems he only knew him as Conrad Meyer," he continued. Then he said, "We're going to do a psychological exam before he gets in front of a judge. I almost feel sorry for the man . . ." He trailed off.

Detective Snyder found himself agreeing with Mitchell. "He is a loose cannon" was all he could say. "Anything on Leavell?" he wanted to know.

Heaving a sigh, Mitchell had to admit to him, a note of frustration in his voice, "No, nothing."

Steve Leavell rolled over on the narrow, lumpy couch. He could hear his cousin and his wife arguing in their bedroom again. Misty didn't want him here. He didn't want to be here either. He had only been here a few days and he already had a job working in the same mechanic shop his cousin worked in. He just needed to get a paycheck and he would get a place of his own. The arguing was driving him crazy.

Finally deciding that he was going to spend all the money he had left from the bank robbery and move out sooner instead of later, he rolled over again and managed to get a little sleep.

During his lunch break the next day, he looked through the apartment ads and found one he thought he could afford. Realizing he hadn't checked his old phone for messages in days, he turned it on. Then he used his new phone to call about the apartment while he waited for everything to load on his old phone.

When a woman answered the phone, he talked to her at length about the apartment. It was still available and he could afford it.

Deciding to rent it sight unseen, he asked if she would hold it for him until he got off work and could swing by the rental office and pay the deposit and the first month's rent.

The apartment was his! He just had to go there after work and pay the landlord. It would leave him with very little money, and no furniture, but he was pretty sure Misty wouldn't mind him eating supper with them until he got his check.

Steve went back to work with a spring in his step. His life was looking up. Coming to Washington state had been a smart move. And he really didn't care how bad the apartment might turn out to be. He was going to stay there and work, and save up his money till he could do better. Who knows, maybe he could even find a few small side jobs like he'd had with Arnold.

It was then he remembered that he had turned his old phone on. He quickly checked it for messages. Only seeing one from Matt, and not caring what it said, he shut the phone off again and took out the battery. Had anyone tracked him here because he forgot about that phone being on? He hoped not. He really hoped not.

There was a knock on Mitchell's office door. "Enter," he barked. It had been a long day. He really just wanted to go home.

"Sir. We found Leavell." Officer Trey Smith stood just inside his door.

Mitchell gave the man his full attention. He was out of his chair and following Officer Smith down the hallway as fast as his feet would carry him. Suddenly, he wasn't tired anymore. "Where is he?" he wanted to know.

Smith never even glanced back over his shoulder when he responded, "Washington state." Then he pushed open the door to a room full of electronic equipment.

Staring at the computer screen, Mitchell saw the red blip in the middle of the map. "Bellevue, huh?" Mitchell breathed.

"Their local blues have already been contacted," Smith stated. "They're on their way to pick him up." There was a smile in his voice.

"We don't really have anything to charge him with yet," Mitchell reminded his man. "We can still ask him a whole lot of questions."

The workday was finally over. Steve Leavell punched the time clock and headed for his car. Opening the trunk, he tossed his work coveralls, gloves, and safety goggles in. Glancing around, not seeing anyone paying any attention to him, he unzipped the side pocket of his backpack and pulled out a fistful of twenties. "That should be enough to cover the rent," he said to himself, slamming the lid and heading for the driver's side.

The first sign he had of any trouble was the low whistle. Then: "That's a whole lot of cash for a mechanic to be toting around in a backpack."

When he turned around, Steve saw six undercover cops surrounding him. *Where had they been hiding?* he wondered.

Frustrated and more than a little angry with himself for forgetting to shut his phone off, Steve could only put his hands up in surrender. Still, he thought to himself, *Another half hour from now and I would have been broke and, maybe, stayed free.*

"Mitchell here." The man knew the call was from the authorities in Bellevue, Washington. He prayed the news was good. His prayers were answered. He quickly made the call to Centerville, Illinois.

"Snyder here. Do you have good news for me, Mitchell?"

"Yes, I do," Mitchell was happy to report. "Authorities in Bellevue, Washington, caught up with Leavell." He continued the conversation, informing Detective Snyder, "He had a fistful of twenties that still had the band on them from one of the banks in Pittsburgh." Mitchell actually chuckled.

Snyder sounded like he was swallowing back a laugh himself when he responded, "Leavell will be going away for a very long time, then."

EPILOGUE

———†———

"Detective Snyder! Come in, please." Marcus's surprise registered in his voice as the detective walked into the parsonage living room. Lori appeared in the kitchen doorway, a dishtowel in her hand and questions in her eyes.

"I wanted to share the good news with you both in person," Snyder began without preamble. "We have Steve Leavell in custody now too." Then, a huge smile reaching his eyes, he told his friends, "It's over."

Lori had come up beside her husband, and now his arm wrapped itself around her waist and pulled her close. Tears sprang from her eyes and Marcus heaved in a breath. He felt like it was the first breath he had breathed since last Christmas. "That's wonderful news!" he was finally able to exclaim.

Wiping her eyes and laughing, Lori finally found her voice too. "Yes! Yes it is." Then, grinning, first at Marcus then at the detective, she suggested, "Let's celebrate! I have apple pie and coffee, and I really want you to join us." Then she added, for Marcus, "It's Tonya's recipe."

"Detective, if you walk away from this, you are a very silly man," Marcus informed him and slapped him on the back as Lori took his hand and led him to their kitchen table.

Not being a silly man, Derrick Snyder allowed himself to be pulled into his pastor's kitchen. It would be the first of many times to come.

CPSIA information can be obtained
at www.ICGtesting.com
Printed in the USA
LVHW040341260820
664160LV00004B/473